THE FREEDOM *of* JENNY

JULIE BURTINSHAW

RAINCOAST BOOKS
Vancouver

Raincoast Books gratefully acknowledges the ongoing support of the Canada
Council for the Arts, the British Columbia Arts Council and the Government
of Canada through the Book Publishing Industry Development Program
(BPIDP).

Edited by Lynn Henry
Cover and interior design by Teresa Bubela

Library and Archives Canada Cataloguing in Publication

Burtinshaw, Julie, 1958-
    The freedom of Jenny / Julie Burtinshaw.
ISBN 1-55192-839-6
    1. African Americans—British Columbia—Fiction.
    I. Title.
PS8553.U69623F74 2005 C813'.6 C2005-903574-9

LIBRARY OF CONGRESS CATALOGUE NUMBER: 2005928390

Raincoast Books   In the United States:
9050 Shaughnessy Street   Publishers Group West
Vancouver, British Columbia   1700 Fourth Street
Canada V6P 6E5   Berkeley, California
www.raincoast.com   94710

At Raincoast Books we are committed to protecting the environment and to
the responsible use of natural resources. We are working with our suppliers
and printers to phase out our use of paper produced from ancient forests.
This book is printed with vegetable-based inks on 100% ancient-forest-free
paper (100% post-consumer recycled), processed chlorine- and acid-free.
For further information, visit our website at www.raincoast.com/publishing.
We are working with Markets Initiative (www.oldgrowthfree.com) on this
project.

Printed in Canada by Webcom.

10 9 8 7 6 5 4 3 2 1

To Kathleen

"Old master, don't cry for me,
For I am going to Canada
Where colored men are free."

— from "Songs of Freedom" (traditional)

CONTENTS

Oppression! I have seen thee, face to face,
And met thy cruel eye and cloudy brow;
But thy soul-withering glance I fear not now —
For dread to prouder feelings doth give place
Of deep abhorrence! Scorning the disgrace
Of slavish knees that at thy footstool bow,
I also kneel — but with far other vow
Do hail thee and thy horde of hirelings base: —
I swear, while life-blood warms my throbbing veins,
Still to oppose and thwart, with heart and hand,
Thy brutalizing sway — till Afric's chains
Are burst, and Freedom rules the rescued land, —
Trampling Oppression and his iron rod:
Such is the vow I take — so help me God!

WILLIAM LLOYD GARRISON (Editor: *The Liberator*)
JANUARY 1, 1831

In July 1844, twelve years after William Lloyd Garrison became the first white man to publicly denounce slavery in the United States, Hannah Estes, born free in Madagascar and enslaved in Clay County, Missouri, gave birth to her third child. The fair-skinned Jenny became a baby sister for two-year-old Joseph and four-year-old Agnes.

SLAVE:

14th century, from Medieval Latin *sclavus,* a captive;
a person who is the legal property of another or others
and is bound to absolute obedience.

EPILOGUE

*B*ecause his new baby daughter was born on a Tuesday, Howard Estes, husband of the slave girl Hannah and chattel of Tom Estes, did not see her until early Saturday morning. Still, he felt no resentment and made no complaints. Howard knew that his master, proprietor of his body and donor of his last name (as was the custom), was a good man. He'd never raised a finger against Howard or anyone else under his roof, and few slaves in Clay County, Missouri enjoyed the privilege of weekend visits with their families, as Howard did.

Moreover, nobody exercised control over Howard's dreams or the people he loved.

When Howard set off that Saturday morning, he walked lightly down the dusty road, taking care to avoid eye contact with the well-heeled white people who kept to the wooden side-walk. He'd learned at a young age that it was wiser to sidestep trouble than to court it.

When Howard first laid eyes on baby Jenny, his stomach did two slow flips. Did proof of his deepest fears lay in the tiny, pale finger curled around his own? Had his beautiful wife been forced to lie with her owner, Charles Leopold, the German baker?

"Hannah ..." he said. He let the sentence hang, lacking the courage to give voice to his terror, but his eyes spoke for him. Hannah watched him and knew his suspicions. She had always been able to recognize the best and the worst of his thoughts.

She squeezed Howard's hand and reassured him that the baby's light skin reflected her own mixed ancestry. "Howard, you know my granddaddy was a white man, and it's bound to show up somewhere in one of our children."

"I would have loved her no matter what," Howard said, hoping it was the truth. He ran his rough finger along their baby's tiny turned-up nose and kissed his exhausted wife on her damp forehead.

Hannah smiled weakly. She knew her husband was a good man, even if he doubted himself. She also knew that if it weren't for Mrs. Leopold's watchful guard over the master, this baby could have easily belonged to the yellow-haired German.

Of course, she'd kill the master before she'd ever let him touch her.

Howard stayed with his family all day Saturday and Sunday, as was his custom. He took four-year-old Agnes and two-year-old Joseph, his older children, out to play in the hot Missouri sunshine. When little Jenny wasn't at her mother's breast, he cradled her in his strong brown arms, and sang the same lullabies his momma had sang to him long ago on the magical shores of Africa where he'd been born. He cooked up a batch of fresh cornmeal bread and butchered a chicken, showing Agnes how to dip it in hot water to make the feathers come off more easily.

Before he left on Sunday night, he whispered in Hannah's ear, "I've started to put away a little money so that our grandchildren will be born into freedom."

Hannah nodded, pretended delight, even though the concept of freedom seemed so foreign to her, and so unimportant. Let Howard dream, she thought. Freedom costs a lot of money, more money than an indentured slave with a family of four could ever hope to raise.

Hannah knew a bit about emancipation. Ike Leopold, who was one of the few black men in the Leopold household who knew the alphabet, would sometimes sit with her in the kitchen while she worked, and read her articles out of *The Liberator*. Someone always managed to sneak William Garrison's abolitionist newspaper into the house, so Hannah knew about the north where slavery was illegal and a black man could own a home and get paid for his work just like anyone else.

"William Garrison says that the American Declaration of Independence is written for everyone, not just white people," Ike had told her one day. He glanced toward the kitchen door to make sure the mistress wasn't lurking nearby to catch him in this act of treason before he continued. He read carefully using his finger as a compass to negotiate his way through the sometimes-unfamiliar vocabulary. When necessary, he stopped to sound out the bigger words. "Listen to this: 'All men are created equal, and endowed by their Creator with certain inalienable rights — among which are life, liberty and the pursuit of happiness.'"

"All men might be created equal," Hannah replied, swatting Ike with her dishcloth, "but I see it is me working and you reading, and it's usually me cooking and you eating. Where do us women fit into all of this?" She'd laughed good-naturedly and shooed him out of her kitchen.

Still, part of her wanted to believe it was true.

Unconsciously, she hummed a few lines from an old song that she'd learned as a little girl:

O pity, all ye sons of Joy,
The little wand'ring Negro-boy.

OPPRESSION:

Cruel use of authority or power to control people;
prolonged harsh or cruel treatment or control.

CHAPTER ONE

*L*ittle Jenny was put to work as soon as her plump legs were strong enough to support her stout body, and her long fingers deft enough to hold a dishcloth in one hand and a plate in the other. While her older brother Joseph toiled outdoors tilling the soil, planting seeds and harvesting the vegetables with the other little boys, her sister Agnes cleaned the Leopold house, gathering the soiled sheets, pillowcases, and clothing for Momma to wash. Jenny perched on a chair in front of the deep enamel sink drying dishes, or mixing flour and eggs until they were just the right consistency for biscuits.

Jenny knew that Momma loved her and Agnes and Joseph more than anything. Because of this, Momma was very strict with all three of them. They went to church every Sunday and sat in the back pews with the other slaves. Every night before bedtime they knelt on the wooden floor beside their cots and prayed to the Lord. Jenny tried her best to be humble and obedient because Momma warned her that if she didn't behave, Mrs. Leopold wouldn't hesitate to sell her to one of the shifty-eyed slave-breakers who passed through Clay County on their regular rounds of southern towns and villages.

"Either you do as you're told, or I'll put you in my pocket," Mrs. Leopold often threatened. Jenny believed her. She was pretty sure that when God gave out hearts, he somehow missed Mrs. Leopold. Nobody dared to cross her. Even the much kinder Mr. Leopold rarely stood up to his wife.

Everyone knew there was nothing more terrifying than slave-breakers — not even the Devil himself. "If you see one of those evil men, turn and run," Momma warned Jenny. "They are just as likely to grab you off the street as they are to buy you. If that happens, you'll disappear onto a cotton plantation and never see anyone in your family again."

Momma had seen many slaves bought and sold by the mistress of the household, sometimes on a cruel whim, sometimes out of spite or bad temper. She'd seen small children dragged from their mothers' arms, and old men turned out on the street just because they could no longer work as hard as when they were young.

Still, Jenny's earliest memories of working beside Momma in the Leopold's big modern kitchen were happy ones. If there were no white folks around, Momma sang. She had a strong, clear voice and Jenny supposed that on the Sabbath Momma's voice might carry all the way to the front of the church where the white folks sat in their fancy Sunday best. Momma sang songs about God and freedom, and sometimes if she was in a good mood, she told Jenny stories about her own childhood on the exotic island of Madagascar.

Madagascar, Jenny realized at a young age, was the best place in the world. Madagascar sat like a priceless jewel in the middle of a turquoise ocean and its rain forest was home to a thousand exotic creatures. The people spoke a strange, beautiful language and everybody got along together. Island life was superior to landlocked life. Jenny dreamed that one day she would live surrounded by the sea.

Momma talked about all kinds of things, but there were two subjects that were strictly taboo. The first was how she came to be in Clay County, Missouri, so far from the jungles of Madagascar. The only thing she'd say about that long-ago journey across the ocean on the slave ship was, "Your grandparents are buried somewhere between here and there — buried at sea," and she'd turn her head so that Jenny wouldn't see the tears welling up in her luminous eyes.

Jenny spent a great deal of time wondering what it meant to be "buried at sea." Did it mean that somehow Granny and Grandpa's bodies, their flesh long fallen from the bone, rested beneath the ocean floor? Or did it mean that Momma's parents weren't buried at all, but consumed by sharks, their bones decomposing on some faraway shore? She never dared to ask, and Momma never told.

The second subject that Momma would never discuss was how she got the thick angry welts that criss-crossed her back and arms like purple rivers on a dark landscape. When Momma was extra tired, she rubbed her scars, and her face creased and she sighed without even knowing she was doing it.

Of all the stories that Momma told, Jenny favored the one

she called The Moses of our Race. "Tell me about Harriet Ross," she'd beg. No matter how many times she'd heard *that* story, she longed to hear it again.

Harriet Ross was the kind of woman Jenny wanted to grow into.

Whenever Jenny asked for that story, Momma would peer around the room to make sure none of the Leopolds were within earshot. Than she'd smile and say, "Jenny, I must've told you that story a hundred times already."

"Just tell it one more time," Jenny would beg. She would turn her big-toothed smile on her momma and wait.

On occasion Momma dove into the story immediately, but most of the time she'd refuse to say a word about it until her youngest had settled properly into a chore. That's how Jenny learned to sew and to knit. Often the brittle broom straws that seconded as knitting needles snapped in half when she'd only done two or three rows and Jenny cried out in frustration, "I need real wooden knitting needles like Agnes has."

"Not until you can knit properly," Momma said. "Now stop wailing and get back to work."

Although Momma never hit any of her children, not even Jenny who was by far the most obstinate, she put an end to histrionics quickly with threats of slave-breakers and hints of things even worse. Jenny sensed Momma didn't like doing this, scaring the three of them, but some things were a matter of survival — "Better to scare you with the truth than to lose you," she'd say.

So Jenny extracted the broken straw from the wool and replaced it with a fresh one out of the broom. She knew she had to learn patience, and learn it soon. In a few months Mrs. Leopold was having another baby, her fifth, and even though Jenny was barely seven, she'd been told that it would be her responsibility to care for five-year-old Anna, leaving Mrs. Leopold free to look after the new baby.

Anna was excited to be getting a little girl slave of her own, and Jenny was excited because it meant she would spend more time in the library and less time in the kitchen.

Jenny didn't mind Anna, who was more like her father than her mother. Sometimes Anna put on airs and acted bossy and stuck-up, but most of the time she treated Jenny almost as a friend. Once she even complimented Jenny by saying: "Your skin is so white, I forgot you were a slave for a moment!" That was the first time Jenny realized she looked different from her brother and sister. If it wasn't for her thick, curly hair, she could pass for a white person.

Momma said Jenny's pale complexion was a curse — she looked more white than black. Some folks might see this as a good thing, but Momma said that Jenny wouldn't fit in comfortably in any world. Jenny hoped she was wrong.

UNDERGROUND RAILROAD:
A secret network of safe houses and transportation
established to help fugitive slaves escape from the
southern U.S. to Canada and the Free States of the
American North in the years before the Civil War.

CHAPTER TWO

*M*omma dipped Anna Leopold's delicate silk dress in and out of the steaming water. Jenny watched her from her perch on the stool. She knew that washday was as close to Satan's inferno as Momma ever wanted to get. Beads of sweat dripped off Momma's face and ran down her proud neck, soaking the back of her dress. "Lord, Jenny," she said in a worn voice, "it must be a hundred degrees in here."

On Tuesday nights, Joseph brought the wood and kindling in so everything would be ready for Momma in the morning. Wednesday was laundry day. And every Wednesday Momma got up before dawn to stoke the fire that burned beneath the fifty-gallon laundry barrel.

The Leopolds generated enough laundry in seven days to keep Momma, Agnes and Jenny busy from early Wednesday morning to late Wednesday night. Sometimes Jenny worried the scrubbing and rinsing and ironing was too much for her mother. Out of the corner of her eye, Jenny saw Momma rub the place between her shoulders where her back ached the most, all the while concentrating on the little mistress' dress. She took great care with the expensive material, even though she'd said to Jenny a hundred times that she thought it was ridiculous for a five-year-old girl to be dressed in such finery when her poor little girls were clad only in threadbare, heavily mended cotton frocks.

Some slaves in the other houses allowed their children to try on the family's clothes when the family was away, and the really daring slaves donned the mistress' gowns themselves, but Momma didn't allow it. She didn't want her daughters to become vain or envious. Besides, she couldn't risk them being taken from her.

Like Momma had been taken from her own momma and daddy, thought Jenny. Momma had to teach her children to be so good they were invisible.

Jenny jumped off her stool and took the newly cleaned frock from her momma. It was her job to hang it on the drying rack, but before she did, she held it up against her body and pirouetted across the small, hot room. Momma frowned at Jenny. "Hang that dress up and get back to your knitting," she said.

"Yes, Momma." Jenny tried her best to be obedient like her sister and brother, but doing the bidding of others didn't come easily to her. She hung up the dress and returned to her stool and her knitting. She'd somehow dropped three stitches. Exasperated, she unraveled the row and started again.

"Show some patience, Jenny. The only person I've ever known to be as fidgety and curious as you is your daddy."

"Momma, tell me about Harriet Ross."

Jenny's request was met with a sigh. "Joseph and Agnes are content with stories from the Bible, but not you. I'll tell you the story again, but before I begin I want you to apologize for your behavior in church on Sunday."

Last Sunday at church Jenny had squirmed through the whole service, until fussy Mrs. Turner from three houses down had turned in her pew and shot a warning glance at the whole family.

"Hush, girl," Momma had said to Jenny.

Jenny pouted through the rest of the service. When they'd left church and were out of earshot of the congregation, Jenny turned to her father. "God would never say such a thing, would he, Daddy." It was a statement, not a question.

The Reverend had taken the text of his sermon from *Colossians*, verse three, chapter 22: "Servants, be obedient to them that are your masters according to the flesh, with fear and trembling, in singleness of your heart, as unto Christ."

"Well, it's possible to twist words." Daddy smiled down at Jenny and patted her on her head warmly. "And no man can twist words as well as the pious Reverend Hansen. I personally don't think that not obeying your earthly master is the same thing as not obeying your heavenly master."

"Stop encouraging her," Momma snapped. "It won't do her any good in the long run."

Daddy always said that Jenny was the reason he was saving up to buy their freedom. She'd end up in the hands of a slave-breaker if he didn't take them all away from the south.

"I'm sorry, Momma," Jenny said now, eager to hear the story

of Harriet Ross. "Next week I'll sit still and listen to everything that horrible Reverend Hansen says."

Momma sighed and squeezed the last drops of clean water out of another of Anna's silk dresses. She hung it over the drying rack by the stove.

"That's my job," Jenny said.

"I don't want to distract you from your knitting," Momma replied. She reached for the next soiled garment. "Harriet Ross," she began, "was born into slavery in 1820 in Maryland, Virginia. Her parents were pure African blood, stolen from Africa ..."

"Just like you were stolen from Madagascar," Jenny interrupted without thinking. A look of sadness passed over Momma's face, and Jenny regretted her words. "I'm sorry," she said. "I won't say another word."

"Don't make promises you can't keep, child. Anyway, Harriet's skin was dark and beautiful like a deep-jungle panther's. Even when she was a little nip of a girl, her master beat her mercilessly until one day when she was twelve years old she decided she'd had enough. In a blind fury, she turned on him and hit him back."

Jenny's hands stopped. Her thoughts wandered back through time. She put down her knitting and tried to imagine how brave a girl would have to be to hit her master back.

"Where did she hit him?" Jenny asked.

"It really doesn't matter." Momma, who knew her daughter well, added, "It was a stupid thing to do. Her enraged master sold her that very day to a slave-breaker. He did terrible, unmentionable things to her and then he left her for dead, but she didn't die and Mr. Leopold bought her for a song and vowed to nurse her back to health. He said even an animal shouldn't be treated that way and he put her under my care. Mrs. Leopold wasn't too pleased, but even an ornery woman like her has to obey her husband. I remember when Harriet came here, she could hardly walk — she was bruised and bleeding but still defiant." Momma lowered her voice, remembering how very angry, how ill, how close to death and yet full of life the young Harriet had been.

"She told me that the slave-breaker beat her daily, but she refused to submit. One day, he pulled out his gun and threatened to shoot her dead if she defied him one more time. Harriet fixed her gaze on him and though he tried to stare her down, she didn't flinch. If she was afraid for her life, she hid it well.

"'Go ahead,' she told him. 'Shoot and be done with it. I would rather die than live such a life.'

"He smiled, but his eyes were full of hate and then he cocked his gun, took aim and shot her in the knees. Two shots. In that action, he condemned his soul to Hell. 'Useless slave cripple,' he taunted. 'Now let's see you fight back.'

"When Mr. Leopold saw the condition Harriet was in, he did the right thing, the Christian thing, and bought her. In some ways he is a good white man — always remember that. He handed her over to me. It was my job to nurse her back to health, and I did it. When she was able, Harriet worked hard and she was a good slave, but ... she wanted more. As soon as she was well enough and she had opportunity, she escaped to the north and married a free African black named John Tubman."

"How'd she meet him?" Jenny asked.

"Jenny, you always ask the same question and I always give you the same answer: I don't know. Anyway, she and her man started the Underground Railroad and pretty soon she got the nickname, *The Moses of her People.* She conducted nineteen trips to the north with runaway slaves. That was over three hundred people. Pretty soon the whites put a bounty of forty-thousand dollars on her head."

Forty thousand dollars was more money than Jenny could imagine. She knew that the Underground Railroad wasn't a real railroad and that Harriet Ross hadn't actually been a train conductor. She imagined the young woman leading the terri-fied slaves from house to house in the dead of the night, and then smuggling them across the Canadian border to freedom.

For a long time, Jenny had thought Freedom was a place — like heaven — but Daddy taught her that it was more than that. It was something bigger. It was a State of Being — being who you wanted, without anyone but your own conscience telling you how to act or how to think.

"Did they catch her?" Jenny said.

"You know they didn't. Now quiet. I hear someone coming. You get back to your knitting, girl. No more stories today."

Ten-year-old Agnes entered the kitchen, carrying a bucket of dirty water and a mop. She flopped down beside Jenny and gave her knitting a critical glance. "You know Momma will give you real wooden knitting needles when you learn to knit properly. You keep dropping stitches. Why don't you pay more attention to what you are doing?"

Jenny regarded her older sister. As much as she loved Agnes, they were different. Agnes had a frail build, unlike anyone else in the family, and Agnes accepted her place in the Leopold house; she did her work without complaining. Unlike Jenny, she didn't envy Joseph his time in the sunshine or the relative freedom being a boy gained for him.

Long ago Jenny had learned the futility of arguing with Agnes. Instead, she replied, "I can knit, but it's not all I do with my time."

Agnes glanced warily at Momma. "I know what you do," she whispered, "and if Momma caught you book-learning, she'd be some mad."

"Daddy says everyone should know how to read," Jenny shot back.

"That may be true, but you shouldn't be going near the Leopolds' books. Mrs. Leopold would beat you within an inch of your life if she caught you."

"That's because Mrs. Leopold can't read," Jenny retorted.

The tinkling of the kitchen bell ended the conversation. Jenny threw her knitting down and leapt out of her chair. "That'll be Anna needing me in the library."

"Slow down, child. Pick up your knitting, straighten out your frock and walk, don't run to your next chore." Momma sounded mad, but Jenny caught her secret smile. Momma knew Jenny loved the library where the Leopold children did their home-work and music lessons. Although she'd never admit it, she was proud of her daughter's burning desire to read and do numbers.

"You can tell me the story of "the Moses of our people" again later," Jenny shouted, and disappeared out the door before her mother or sister had time to caution her to slow down.

"She doesn't know her place," Agnes said, emptying the bucket of dirty water out the back door.

"Or, she *does*," Momma said. "Agnes, don't throw the water so close to the stoop."

In the library, blonde-haired, blue-eyed Anna Leopold sat quietly staring out the large bay window that faced the back garden. Her books lay open and unread in front of her. Jenny could see she was miles away from the task at hand. If Jenny were asked her opinion of Anna, she would say, "I guess I like her but she's a spoiled, bratty girl and none too bright to boot."

"Good, you're here, Jenny. I'm having a hard time with my arithmetic." Anna slid the book and pencil across the table. The pencil fell to the floor, where Anna left it. "You do it, and sharpen my pencil." Numbers always put Anna in a surly mood.

"Where are the others?" Jenny knew the penalty for doing Anna's work could be high. It was against the law for a slave to be educated. She took extreme care never to be caught.

"They've gone to grandmother's for afternoon tea. I had to stay behind to finish my homework." Anna's little pink lips formed a pout. "I hate school."

Jenny sharpened the pencil, sat down across the table from Anna and went to work on the simple arithmetic. "Look, it's easy: If you have ten apples and you take away three and a half apples, you are left with six and a half." She handed Anna the pencil so she could write down the answer. "I'd give anything to go to school," she sighed.

Anna laughed. "Slaves don't go to school. Even if their skin is white, their hearts are black. Don't be stupid. It's against the law to teach slaves. You're lucky I don't tell."

Jenny wasn't hurt and she wasn't afraid. Anna wouldn't tell, because Anna needed her. Anyway, she'd grown up listening to this kind of talk. *Harriet Ross knew how to read and write*, she thought. *My hero was born a slave and now she is free.*

Daddy had promised Jenny that one day she'd be free too. He'd even got her to read aloud articles from William Garrison's paper, *The Liberator*, so Jenny knew there were white people who didn't believe in slavery either. William Garrison was from the north and he had probably met Harriet Ross.

"I am lucky," Jenny agreed easily with Anna. But she averted her eyes because Momma said eyes are the windows to the soul. It wouldn't serve any purpose to get caught lying or to make Anna Leopold angry.

Jenny worked through the equations quickly, directing Anna to count out the answers on her fingers before writing them down. Anna seemed preoccupied and lazier than usual. She fell asleep twice and Jenny shook her awake.

When they were finished, Anna demanded they go out into the garden to get some air. "I don't feel well," she whined.

Jenny followed her obediently, listening with only half an ear to her dull talk. She winced when Anna sat down in the dust because she knew Momma would have to launder yet another dress in the hot kitchen.

"Let's keep walking," she suggested, but Anna wouldn't budge.

"I don't feel so good."

Jenny looked at Anna, really looked at her, for the first time that day. Anna's cheeks were flushed and her eyes watery and pink. She placed her hand on the blonde girl's forehead; she was burning up.

"You're on fire," Jenny said. "Come on, I'm bringing you to my momma."

"I can't. I'm too tired," Anna whispered.

Jenny pulled Anna to her feet and led her slowly around the back of the house and into the kitchen where Momma was stirring the laundry with the big stick reserved especially for that purpose. The heat in the kitchen made breathing difficult. Jenny noticed the back of her momma's dress was drenched in sweat. Momma didn't stop what she was doing, although she greeted Anna politely.

"Hello, Miss Anna. Have you come looking for biscuits and cake?"

Anna leaned heavily against Jenny. She coughed. "My throat hurts," she murmured.

"Momma," said Jenny and the alarm in her voice caused her mother to turn around.

"Lord," Momma said. She was staring at Anna, but feeling terror for her own child. "You don't look well at all."

Anna looked up at her with glazed eyes and sank to the floor.

SCARLET FEVER:

An infectious bacterial fever characterized by inflammation of the nose, throat and mouth, and a red rash called "scarlatina."

CHAPTER THREE

*J*enny's father, Howard Estes, stood at the back door of the Leopold mansion and squinted at the messily scrawled note stuck on the heavy oak panels. He couldn't remember the last time he'd found the door closed on a day so hot the ground burned the soles of your feet, and he wondered if the note offered an explanation. Unsure of what to do, he knocked softly. After all, it was Saturday and he had a right to see his family. And today was a special Saturday. He had news, news that would change their lives. Why weren't the children playing outside? Why were all the blinds drawn upstairs? He knocked again.

"Who is it?" Jenny called from the other side of the door.

Daddy smiled when he heard her voice. "What are you up to? It's your daddy, girl. Who else are you expecting on a Saturday? Open up the door."

"Didn't you see the notice?" Jenny asked, then immediately regretted it. Daddy couldn't read and he wasn't proud of it. "The Leopolds have scarlet fever," she said quickly. "The doctor says nobody is allowed in the house. We are under quarantine." She let the big word roll off her tongue — a new word and she liked the way it sounded. "That means …"

"I know what it means," Daddy said in a faint voice. Scarlet fever, and his family locked in there with the lot of them. "What about your momma and you and Joseph and Agnes? Are any of you sick?"

"No. Momma says we are stronger than white folk. Momma is upstairs with the baby, but she says to tell you to wait for her in the tool shed. She'll be along as soon as she can."

Daddy looked around nervously. "Keep your voice down or you'll be overheard."

Jenny smiled. "Don't worry. The Leopolds are all in bed behind closed doors."

"Well, you stay as far away from them as you can. Hear me, girl?"

"Don't worry, Daddy. I'll be fine." Jenny blew him a kiss and closed the window.

The deadly scarlet fever cut a swath of sore throats, high temperatures, itchy rashes and gasping breaths through the Leopold household, but it didn't bother Jenny. Because the mistress and her family were confined to bed rest, she had the run of the house — more importantly, unhindered access to the library. Momma rushed about from sick room to sick room with armloads of clean towels, dry clothes and buckets of hot water, leaving a trail of orders behind her. Her tight-lipped silence and worried expression frightened Jenny but she did her best to ignore it.

Now Jenny waited outside the baby's room for Momma to come out. "Daddy's waiting for you in the tool shed," she whispered.

"I don't know how long it will be until I can leave the house," Momma said. "Take your Daddy a tall glass of iced tea and tell him I'll be there as soon as I can."

Jenny did as she was told, before returning to help Agnes make soup for the sick family. At ten years of age, Agnes was already a good cook. While Jenny chopped up carrots and potatoes, Agnes plucked the chicken, separated the meat from the bones and started the stock. The sisters worked steadily, humming together happily and the soup was soon simmering on the stovetop.

Daddy waited for two long hours before Momma, Jenny trailing behind her, was able to join him out back. As they entered the tool shed, Jenny noticed the concerned look on her father's face and she knew he was afraid for all of them. Momma looked exhausted, dark circles framed her eyes. She dropped heavily onto the hard wooden bench, the only piece of furniture in the tool shed. Neither of her parents noticed Jenny's figure in the doorway. She made herself small so they wouldn't tell her to go away and busy herself.

Daddy put his arms around Momma and held her close to him. "You're not sick too, are you?"

She shook her head wearily.

"They working you too hard?"

"Not according to Mrs. Leopold." Momma rolled her eyes. "If I were working too hard, I'd be dead, according to that woman.

At least none of our children are struck down by the fever — yet."

"God willing, they won't be," said Daddy. He paused. Jenny saw hesitation in his expression. She knew that he didn't fear much, but he feared Momma. What was he holding back?

"I know this might not be the best time, but it's the only time I have. I'm here with good news for you," Daddy began. He'd wondered how to introduce the topic that had dominated his thoughts for the last three days. He knew his wife would always support him, but he also realized that this time, it wouldn't be easy. He took a big breath and dove in. "It's not too much longer before we'll have enough money to buy our freedom and go west."

"Howard, you're such a dreamer. Where's a black man going to get that kind of money?" Jenny heard the irritation in her mother's voice. "At least I know where Jenny gets it from — always thinking about tomorrow, when today is all we really have."

"Hope is not a bad quality in a person, Hannah. I know I've been saying this — talking about freedom — for a lot of years, but this time I mean it." When Momma didn't say anything, he continued. "There's a gold rush out in the free state of California, and they're in need of cattle in a big way. Mr. Estes is sending out five hundred head and I'm to go along."

In the shadow of the doorway, Jenny hugged herself to stop from jumping up and down in excitement.

Daddy couldn't contain his enthusiasm. He stood up and began to pace back and forth across the rough floor of the shed, but Jenny saw fear in her mother's eyes. She held her breath. What would Momma say?

"I have indenture papers — a contract that says if I make the trip, he'll grant me my freedom papers. It'll cost twenty-six hundred dollars. Some I'll earn driving the cattle west and the rest I'll make in California in the mines. Hannah, we're going to be free people." Daddy sat down beside Momma and looked her directly in the eye. "Free." Jenny sensed a mixture of apprehension and passion in his voice. What if she said no?

"How long will you be gone?" Momma asked. She didn't wait for an answer. "What if you never return? There are Indians and outlaws and you are just a black man with a dream."

"Six months, maybe longer." Daddy cast his eyes down to the floor.

"How much longer?" Jenny recognized panic in her mother's question. "How much longer, Howard?" Her voice broke and she swallowed hard.

"A year at the outside. I'll spend some time in the gold mines making the money *we* need to buy our freedom. I'll start looking around for a home for us. The children will be able to go to school. Jenny will be allowed to read, without fear of punishment."

Jenny closed her eyes and pressed her back against the door frame. She'd never dared to let herself even dream about attending a school and now it was a real possibility. "Please Lord, make Momma agree," she prayed silently.

"I'm sorry, Howard. I'm tired." Momma closed her eyes. "The Leopold children are on the mend, but until they are completely cured, there's no rest for me, Agnes or even Jenny. And what if our children get the fever?"

Worry lines that hadn't been there a second ago creased Daddy's face. Momma reached over and placed her hand on his cheek. "I know this isn't the right way to send the man you love into the unknown. I know we've talked about this so often before, but I never thought the day would come when you would actually be leaving."

"The day is here. We leave mid-week. Hannah, I don't want to leave you and the children, but if I turn Mr. Estes down, I'll be throwing away our only chance at freedom."

"Turn him down! No." Momma placed her work-worn hand on Daddy's knee, where his pants were torn. "I'll have to mend these before you leave," she said. "I won't hear of you turning him down. Anyway, the sooner you go, the sooner you'll return. You will return, won't you? I'm not going all the way to California without you at my side."

"I'll be back," Daddy promised. "I'll be back to take you and our children to the free state of California, where we can work, the children can go to school and we can walk down the street holding our heads proud."

Momma nodded and smiled, but Jenny saw that her heart was weighed down with worry. "We have an acceptable life here in Clay County," she told Daddy. "Nobody beats us and we have a roof over our heads and plenty of food. I can't help but think of Harriet Ross. She came so close so many times to losing her life for an unknown future. I can't help but think of William Garrison whose fight for freedom cost him his friends and his family. I can't help but think of all of our people who run for the north just to be caught, tortured, maimed and killed.

All those broken families and orphaned children … Be careful, Howard," she said. "Pray to the Lord every day, and watch your back. Mr. Estes may be a kind man, but his skin is white, and white folks are not like us, no matter what they might say to the contrary."

"Mr. Estes' blood and our blood is the same color," replied Daddy. "He's a good man and he's promised to keep the family together until I return. Nobody will be sold. Leopold doesn't own you and the children. Mr. Estes does, so you have no need to worry." He paused. "So I have your blessing?"

Momma knew Howard was right. Originally, she had been sent to the Leopolds to replace a runaway slave, but her short-term placement had turned into a permanent position. Tom Estes remained her rightful owner — a fact she thanked God for every night in her prayers. "You have." Momma nestled into his chest. "You will always have my blessing."

Jenny crept out of the tool shed into the late afternoon sunshine. Behind her, she could hear her mother tell her father to be careful, to eat properly and not to trust other herders on the trail. "I'll pray for you every day," Momma vowed.

Jenny's parents were in the shed for a long time. Finally Momma left and hurried across the dusty yard to the stoop where Jenny, Agnes and Joseph waited for her. "Your father can't spend the weekend here," she told them. "It's against the doctor's orders. Run out to the tool shed. He has something to tell you, but don't tarry. I'll need all of you to help me with the Leopolds."

Daddy broke the news to them quickly, knowing he had to leave before he was discovered. After all, all his children

43

were under quarantine, even if none of them were sick. Joseph reacted to his father's news with uncharacteristic indifference and Agnes too seemed not to care at all, but Jenny was ecstatic. She told Daddy that she thought that a cattle drive all the way across America on the famous Oregon Trail was the most exciting journey a person could undertake. It took all of her willpower to say goodbye and to drag herself from her father's big arms.

After she and Daddy said goodbye, Jenny stood with Momma and Joseph in the back yard until Daddy was long out of sight. Then they all crept back into the kitchen. The house was quiet and dark. Agnes slept at the kitchen table, her head, framed by a mass of curls, resting on her skinny arms. Jenny woke her, and helped her up the stairs to their attic rooms. Momma tucked them all in and kissed them goodnight. She felt their foreheads and put her ear close to their lips.

"Don't worry, Momma," Jenny said.

"Goodnight, Momma," breathed Agnes.

"I love you," said Joseph.

"Please Lord, spare my babies from the fever," Momma whispered as she blew out the lamp. "Keep my children well and watch over their daddy on his journey to the free state of California. Amen."

"Amen," chorused Jenny, Joseph and Agnes.

FREEDOM:

The quality or state of being free; liberation from slavery or restraint or from the power of another.

CHAPTER FOUR

*J*enny stood hidden in the shadows of the towering wooden hutch where Momma kneaded the bread dough every morning. She kept very quiet and listened to her momma arguing with the mistress. Daddy had been gone just over two weeks, and already everything was falling apart. Momma toiled under a blanket of sadness; she moved through her daily chores with stooped shoulders and heavy feet. And now this.

"Mrs. Leopold, surely you could find it in your kind heart to ask the doctor for a little medicine for my Agnes? The fever can spread from one person to another and if Agnes is sick, someone else in your family might catch it." Momma sounded scared.

"Nonsense! Hannah, you're making too much of that girl's behavior. She's not sick. She's lazy, like all Negroes get to be eventually. After all, she's almost eleven now, more woman than child. If she's hot, it's not because she has a fever, it's because she's spent too much time sitting out in the sun and warming herself."

Mrs. Leopold prepared to leave. She gathered up her big skirt in her hand, than changed her mind. "I don't know why you people pretend such affection for your children. You don't see a horse or a dog fretting over their young. Besides, your precious Doctor Henley says it's all a matter of natural selection. The strong slaves will survive, and the weak ones are no use to anybody anyway." She crossed her arms over her large chest and smiled smugly. "Agnes, get up off your behind and go out to the henhouse and collect the eggs. Doctor Henley says eggs are good for Anna while she is recovering."

When Agnes didn't move, Mrs. Leopold glared at her. "Go on, girl. You can't pull the wool over my eyes like you do to your momma."

Sensing Momma's rising frustration, Jenny stepped out from her hiding place behind the hutch. "I'll go," she offered. "I'd be happy to gather eggs for Anna, please, ma'am?"

Jenny despised Mrs. Leopold. She thought Mrs. Leopold was a jealous, hateful woman, but she also knew better than to cross her. She had a cruel streak inside her. That streak was not shared by the master, but Mr. Leopold wasn't home, so Mrs. Leopold would get her own way. On more than one occasion she'd yelled at Jenny, even called her a "dirty little nigger," but only when her husband was out of earshot.

Jenny didn't feel great, either — her throat hurt — but anyone with eyes in their head could see that Agnes was really sick. Her cheeks were flushed, her stare was unfocused and the back of her dress was drenched in sweat. This morning when Agnes woke, her breath had come in shallow gasps, and an angry rash covered most of her small body.

"Hush, Jenny," said Mrs. Leopold. "Hold your tongue."

"We've been nursing your children for weeks," Jenny addressed Mrs. Leopold directly. "It makes sense that we might get sick, too."

"Quiet, child," Momma said. She turned to the mistress. "I'm sorry for my youngest speaking out of turn." She frowned at Jenny. "Jenny, apologize to the mistress, who has always been so good to you."

Momma's words came too late. Mrs. Leopold had turned red as a Missouri sunset. She rushed at Jenny and smacked her hard on the face. "Impudent little slave! What are you doing, eavesdropping on us? One more show of rebellion and you're up for sale." She shook with rage. "Get out of my sight, now!" She raised her hand and struck out at Jenny once more, but Jenny darted out of the way, tears of rage streaming down her face.

"God hates you," she muttered to herself. Daddy always said that the true God, not the one the white preacher spoke for in church on Sundays, loved everyone in spite of the color of his or her skin. Jenny knew that the true God wouldn't have the time of day for a nasty woman like Alice Leopold.

Jenny could see her Momma offering more apologies to the mistress back in the kitchen. She hated to see Momma being so subservient, but in her heart, she knew Momma was doing it for her. She heard Agnes get up slowly from her chair. Footsteps shuffled across the floor, the back door opened and clicked softly shut.

"Humph," said Mrs. Leopold. "Sometimes it's so much work directing you slaves, I wonder if I shouldn't take up the labor myself. Keep those girls under control, Hannah. They're running wild, what with that daddy of theirs taking off across the country and all. No good will come of it, you mark my words."

"Yes, ma'am."

Jenny cringed at the submissiveness in her momma's voice.

"I'll call for you if Anna needs a boiled egg in the night. Be careful, Hannah, or the next slave-breaker who passes the door won't leave empty-handed."

"Yes, ma'am, and thank you."

When Mrs. Leopold had left the kitchen, Jenny went back in. Momma sat at the table, her head cradled in her hands. She didn't acknowledge her daughter except to say, "Go to bed, Jenny, you've caused enough trouble for one day. You are your daddy's girl and there is nothing any of us can do about that."

Jenny walked slowly to the kitchen window and stared out at the rain pounding down on the back stoop. She ran her fingers over the red mark forming on her cheek. Agnes was out there rummaging around the henhouse in her thin frock and bare feet.

"Freedom," she whispered, and pressed her lips against the window.

The hate welling up inside her heart took on a body of its own. It was bigger than her, stronger than her and she felt faint. Without a word to Momma, she took a lit candle off the window ledge and slipped quietly out the back door to find her sister.

The ankle-deep mud pulled at Jenny's feet and the wind threatened to douse the tiny flame, but she held the candle close to her body and sheltered it with her free hand. She made her way across the yard to the henhouse. Inside, Agnes stood before the row of roosts, clutching two eggs. She turned at the sound of Jenny pushing open the door, but said nothing.

"I thought you might need a little light," Jenny said, shocked at how thin Agnes looked in the shadows. "Sit down on the straw. I'll collect the rest of the eggs."

"The mistress will sell you, or worse, if she discovers you're out here," said Agnes. She coughed and struggled for breath.

"She can't do any worse to me," Jenny replied. "I hate her. We have to be patient. Daddy will get us to California and everything will be better, you'll see."

Agnes shook her head, and too tired to argue, dropped to the floor. Jenny shooed a scrawny chicken away and sunk her hand into the straw. She found three eggs. They were warm and smooth in her hands, the mottled brown shells offering curious comfort.

"I had a dream about Daddy," said Agnes in a low, halting voice.

Jenny listened, hearing the effort in each strangled word her sister spoke.

"I dreamt I saw him coming across the field toward home, all dressed up in new clothes. He was smiling, and he had a bag full of presents for us." Agnes coughed again. "My throat hurts so bad …"

"Anyway, he said, 'Where's Agnes?' I said, 'Here I am Daddy,' but he just walked right by me, as if I didn't exist."

Jenny cradled the eggs gently in her palm. Just a tiny bit of pressure and she could crush their delicate shells. A sliver of fear crept up her spine. "Agnes, I don't like that dream."

Before her sister could reply, a brilliant crack of lightning lit up the inside of the henhouse, followed by a roar of thunder rolling across the night sky. The chickens huddled together in the strange light. Outside, the wind picked up and the henhouse door flew open. Jenny stood frozen to the spot. Agnes began to cry softly.

A movement in the doorway caught the girls' attention. They gazed, spellbound, as a creamy white bird no bigger than a swallow hovered in the entrance to the henhouse, its small body inexplicably motionless in the gusting wind. It cocked its head sideways and focused on Agnes before flying in and alighting on her trembling shoulder. Jenny blinked, sure she was imagining the tiny creature. "Agnes," she started, but the bird began to sing and Jenny stopped, captivated by the hauntingly mournful song. Neither Jenny nor Agnes moved a muscle until its song was finished. Then, as quickly as it had appeared, the bird spread its delicate wings and disappeared into the stormy night.

"I've never seen a bird fly at night. Only owls fly at night," Jenny whispered. She felt she had to say something to mask her fear.

Agnes stood up and walked toward the door on unsteady legs. "Don't tell Momma," she said. "Whatever else you do, don't tell Momma."

Jenny left the rest of the eggs — three would be enough for Anna — and followed her sister back to the house. Normally the rain would be a welcome relief from the wet heat that was suffocating Missouri, but tonight Jenny planted herself in front of the great wood stove, and try as she might, she could not warm up.

Momma took Agnes up to bed. Jenny followed her. "I wish your daddy was here," Momma said. "He'd get the medicine we need for my baby."

But a long flat prairie and a high mountain range separated them from Daddy and there was no drug for Agnes.

Upstairs Momma cradled Agnes in her arms, a cold cloth pressed to her daughter's burning skin. Agnes slept fitfully and fought for each breath. Jenny wanted to lie down with her, to keep her warm, but Momma made her stay in doorway. "Keep your distance," she said. "I can't lose two of you."

So Joseph and Jenny watched as Agnes grew weaker and weaker and finally was no more. When her chest stilled, Momma didn't cry. She washed her daughter's small, infection-ravaged body, dressed her in clean clothes and when she'd finished, she lay down beside her.

"Oh Lord, why hast thou forsaken me?"

Outside, the rain continued to wash the dry Missouri ground.

In the morning, Mrs. Leopold had Agnes' body removed from her home.

PRAYER:

A solemn request or entreaty to God or an object of worship; an earnest request or wish.

CHAPTER FIVE

*S*ix weeks turned into six months and doubled to a
year, and still there was no sign of Daddy. Jenny worried
about what would happen if Daddy didn't come home or if he
returned to discover that one of his babies had gone to sleep
forever.

That's how Momma put it: "At least Agnes is safe in the arms
of Jesus," she said in a voice that betrayed no emotion. The spar-
kle in Momma's eyes had vanished the day she lost Agnes.

Clearly, being "safe in the arms of Jesus" was not a good
thing, and Jenny knew that Momma blamed the Leopolds
for not giving Agnes the medicine she needed when the fever
boiled inside her.

Jenny and Joseph recovered from the scarlet fever slowly.
If Momma, with Doctor Henley's help, hadn't insisted on the
doctor giving them medication, they probably wouldn't have
survived either. "If we don't eradicate the fever from your household, it will keep on spreading. We have to medicate everyone,
slaves included," the doctor told Mrs. Leopold sternly.

Mr. Leopold agreed with the doctor. "They should have all been treated from the start," he said to his wife. "If I'd been at home, maybe Agnes would have survived."

"I'm sorry, Hannah," he added when his wife was out of earshot.

Jenny's throat had been so raw she'd been unable to swallow, and she'd been so cold she never thought she'd warm up again, but at least the ugly rash that appeared on her arms and legs had not spread over most of her body like it did with poor Agnes.

Mrs. Leopold had been most concerned about Joseph — a boy slave would be expensive to replace. "Over a thousand dollars I'd have owed Tom Estes," she'd whined, begrudgingly handing over exactly ten doses of the foul-tasting syrupy cure for each of them. "If that doesn't do it, then it's in the Lord's hands." She banged the remedy down on the table in front of Hannah. "And pull yourself together. You still have two children left."

Ever since that terrible night when Agnes closed her eyes and gurgled in her last labored breath, Momma had taken to disappearing for long periods of time, whenever she got the opportunity. One day Jenny decided to follow her. She waited until Momma had slipped out the back door. Then, keeping her distance, she followed Momma across the yard and over the hay field to a dilapidated shack that had perched on the river's edge for as long as she could remember.

When Momma went in and closed the door, Jenny tip-toed over to the broken window, hoisted herself up and peered inside. Momma was kneeling down on the dirt floor; her hands were clasped before her, her head bowed. Jenny saw that she was talking to the Lord. The words were difficult to understand, but even from her safe distance Jenny caught the gist of the prayer. Momma wanted Daddy home safe, she wanted Agnes to be happy in heaven, and most surprisingly, she was ready to go west to California. "And please help me find a place in my heart to forgive Mistress Leopold. I'm having trouble with this, Lord."

Jenny knew from church, and from listening to Momma every single day, that forgiveness was something adults valued, but the reasons why made no sense to her. In the Bible it said that if someone slapped you on the cheek, the best course of action would be to offer him the other cheek. Jenny thought this was perhaps the stupidest thing she'd ever heard. Why should Momma forgive the mistress? Why would she want to?

Jenny couldn't.

On the day that Daddy finally did come home, Joseph spotted him first. Joseph was working in the garden, planting potatoes with the other slave boys, when he looked up and saw the familiar figure striding across the field toward the Leopolds' mansion. Disobedience didn't come easily to Joseph, but today he dropped his shovel and ran out the gate, through the backyard and into the kitchen, not even bothering to wipe his dusty bare feet on the mat.

Jenny and Momma were doing dishes. "Daddy's home!" Joseph cried. "He's coming across the field this second."

Momma dropped a plate and it broke clean down the middle. The three of them flew outside, without bothering to clean up the broken china, and sure enough there was Daddy striding toward them as if he hadn't been gone for over a year.

When Jenny laid eyes on him, it was Agnes' dream in the chicken coop all over again. The sun shone off the shiny material of the new suit he was wearing and he had a bag in his hand — a bag full of presents for all of them.

"It's just like Agnes said," she said to her Momma and brother, and they both gave her a puzzled look. "In her dream, she said she saw Daddy coming home across the field all dressed nicely and carrying a carpet-bag of presents for us." She purposely left out the part about Agnes being invisible to him.

"I've dreamed of this day, and I've dreaded it at the same time," sighed Momma. "He doesn't know ..."

Jenny looked at Momma. She'd aged terribly over the past year. There were flecks of gray in her dark hair, and new lines on her face. Maybe seeing Daddy would make her young again.

As Daddy approached, all the slaves in the Leopolds' house gathered in the back yard, and even the master walked out to join them.

"Well, I'll be damned," he said, "if that nigger didn't make the journey all the way across the country and back."

Daddy was grinning broadly and his white teeth lit up his whole face. Jenny saw the small white bird with the coffee-colored spots that fluttered above him as he made his way toward them. "Agnes is with us," she whispered to herself. "Agnes protected Daddy and made sure he came home."

As Daddy neared, the slaves parted ranks. Some called out his name, welcoming him home, but their greetings were subdued. At first he seemed not to notice, but as he neared

Momma, his smile faded. It didn't take him long to realize that something wasn't right. Maybe it was the way everyone averted their eyes or maybe it was Momma's sad countenance, but by the time Jenny and Joseph rushed forward and threw their arms around his big body, the wide grin on his face had been replaced by a puzzled questioning expression.

Momma didn't hurry forward to greet him. Rather, she moved heavily through the crowd, never taking her eyes off his face. He opened his arms and she fell into them, oblivious to everyone around them. The Leopolds would never approve of such a display of affection.

"Thank God you've returned safely," she murmured, and then she couldn't hold it back any longer and she started to cry. Jenny had never seen her momma cry, and it broke her heart. For close to a year, Momma had kept her pain inside, hidden from Joseph and Jenny.

Howard Estes had had an uneasy feeling in his soul for months. He knew that the little bird that appeared every so often was an omen of some sort — maybe even a guardian angel. He'd been in Panama City the first time it had appeared. He was supposed to be catching a ship — the *Grace Darling* — for the treacherous voyage around Cape Horn, but instead he had contracted malaria. He'd almost died. The bird visited every day — perched on the window ledge of his rented room. On the morning he was strong enough to resume his travels, the bird had disappeared. That afternoon, down at the wharf, he had discovered that the *Grace Darling* had sunk at sea — all hands and passengers were lost.

Whenever he saw the bird, for some reason he thought about Agnes. It was as if she were there beside him all the time, seeing him through his illness to recovery.

Now, seeing his wife's face, he didn't need to ask. The other slaves went back to their chores and Mr. Leopold, who was a good man if his wife wasn't in sight, stepped back into the house, leaving Howard alone with his family.

Jenny wanted to know what was in Daddy's bag, but Joseph took her arm firmly by the elbow and pulled her away. "We'd best get back to our chores, and leave Momma and Daddy to talk things over," he said.

"But … but," Jenny protested.

"No buts," said Joseph. "We've got work to do, and if the mistress catches us all standing around, there'll be trouble for sure."

Daddy stepped forward and wrapped his big arms around Jenny. "You've been a brave girl," he said, and reached into his bag. He pulled out a large doll. She had eyes as brown as Jenny's and long dark hair all the way to her waist. She was dressed in a beautiful blue silk frock, with tiny matching shoes and a matching ribbon in her hair. Jenny didn't think she had ever seen anything so beautiful in her whole life.

"For me?" She didn't dare believe that this doll might be hers to keep. Anna had dolls and so did the other white girls, but Jenny had never dreamed that one day she too might have one.

Daddy grinned. "For you, angel. Now off you go and do as Joseph tells you. I'll talk to Momma for a bit, and on Saturday I'll be over to see you all."

"Thank you, Daddy," said Jenny in a hushed voice. She knew the doll must have cost him a fortune.

Daddy opened his bag and revealed a shiny revolver. "This is for you, Joseph," he said in a quiet voice. "I think it's best not to show it to Momma just yet." He winked. "I thought you might be able to use this when we're all on the Oregon Trail." Joseph couldn't believe his eyes. Blacks weren't allowed to own guns. Daddy closed his bag. "I'll keep it safe until we're gone from this place."

Momma stayed outside with Daddy for a long time. When she returned to the house, Jenny thought she looked happier than she had in weeks and weeks. The old fire, although perhaps not as strong as before, was back in her eyes and she went about her work with a straighter back and a lighter step.

"Are we really going to California to be free?" Jenny whispered to her mother that night after she'd said her prayers and her goodnight to Agnes, who she knew had turned into an angel.

"I believe we are," said Momma. "I believe we are."

Jenny lay down with her new doll hugged close to her chest. Now that Daddy was home, everything seemed right again. Harriet Ross had escaped the chains of slavery, and so would she.

~

While Jenny slept, her momma sat up until dawn. She knew their lives were about to change forever. She prayed they were doing the right thing by leaving Clay County.

EMANCIPATION:

To deliver, transfer or sell from ownership; freeing someone from the control of another.

CHAPTER SIX

*H*oward Estes sat across from the master, Tom Estes, and counted out his money carefully. It was more money than he'd ever held in his hands in his thirty-three years on earth, and with this money he would purchase freedom for his family.

He should have felt joy; instead a growing sense of fear gnawed at his insides. He'd been gone a long time — more than a year — and he'd seen a lot. California might be called a "free state," but as the number of emancipated slaves flowing into the Bay area increased, the white population was becoming more and more restless.

Settling out west wouldn't be as easy as Howard had thought it would be when he used to lie in bed at night and dream about a future out of bondage.

A large black ledger lay open in front of Tom Estes with markings on it — words that Howard could not decipher, and numbers that were the equivalent of his family's market value.

"Well, Howard, the way I see it, you owe me twenty-six hundred dollars: nine hundred for the boy, five for his mother, and six hundred for each girl under eighteen years."

He turned the book around so Howard could read it, but Howard waved it away. "I'm not book-learned," he said, "but the numbers are the ones we agreed on and I've the money in my hand." He paused, looked down and swallowed. "Except, one of my daughters ..." Unable to find the words he needed, he stopped talking altogether.

Tom waited patiently for him to continue. If one of the daughters — probably the oldest one — was in the family way, he wouldn't charge extra. Over the past fourteen months, he'd grudgingly taken a liking to this slave and he didn't mind giving Howard a break on an unborn negro baby. She'd just be another mouth to feed, nothing more.

Howard looked Tom Estes in the eyes and continued. "My eldest, Agnes, she died in the scarlet fever that took the Leopold house just after we left."

"I'm sorry." Tom meant it, although he, like the other slave owners, couldn't understand the attachment these people felt for their children. He suspected at times it might be close to the same thing that he felt for his five sons, but he knew logically that depth of emotion was beyond the Negroes. He lit a cigarette and shifted his eyes. "Well, that saves you six hundred dollars, and that money will come in handy when you're out on the trail."

Beneath the table, Howard clenched and unclenched his fists, fighting to control the anger welling up inside of him.

He had to hold on just a little bit longer. One wrong move and his bid for freedom would be destroyed. "Yes, sir," he replied. He passed the money across the table. "If you wouldn't mind counting it out again for me?"

Relieved to be on more familiar territory, Tom Estes obliged, counting out the bills carefully and handing six hundred dollars back to Howard. "That's it, minus the cost of the slave girl," he said. It annoyed him that Howard didn't seem at all pleased with the money he'd saved. That was the problem with slaves; just a little taste of freedom and they became arrogant and ungrateful. He'd seen it happen before. "When are you planning on leaving?"

Howard had thought about this every day on the six-month journey back to Clay County. The trail was rough and dangerous. They'd need half a year, minimum, and summer lay just around the corner. He'd also need time to get a wagon, a team, food and supplies together. And he'd have to be careful because he didn't have a lot of money left to spend.

"About two months," he said. "I'll need some time to prepare."

"Howard, you were a good man on the trail. Me and the boys are moving another five hundred head west in two weeks' time, come April. You're welcome to come along with me, for wages. Your wife's a good cook, and I'd be willing to pay her for her services. Your children can make themselves useful, and I've got a Conestoga wagon with a wheel broke and an axle needing replacing. You could fix it up for yourselves."

Howard couldn't believe his ears. The money and time it

would save was incalculable, and there was safety in numbers and in traveling with whites.

He smiled a smile that reached his eyes. "Yes, sir," he said. "You won't regret it."

"Good." Tom Estes stood up and reached out his hand to shake Howard's. It wasn't done, shaking hands with coloreds, but Howard was a good man, and he had a hard road ahead of him.

Howard took Tom Estes' hand, surprised at the unusual gesture. Perhaps there was hope after all. William Garrison swore that there were good white men, but there had been times when Howard had doubted.

"Thank you, sir. For everything."

"We leave in two weeks. I'll fix everything with Charles Leopold." Tom nodded and strode out of the room.

Howard sat very still for a long time after the master had departed. Now that he had secured their freedom turning the sweat of his labor into dollars, there was something else, something more important, that he had to do right away. It wouldn't be easy.

He felt old, too old to face what lay ahead. He rose slowly and took his first steps as a free man — a non-indentured man — walking outside into the warm night air. Stars were beginning to appear in the Missouri sky when he turned right toward the church and the cemetery where his beloved Agnes lay six feet under the earth.

It was a fifteen-minute walk from the Estes estate to the Methodist church cemetery, but to Howard it felt like a fifteen-mile walk. Although he'd meant to think only about Agnes, his thoughts kept drifting back to his wife. He'd been shocked when he'd seen Hannah the day he returned. She'd looked dog-tired, moving heavily as if every step cost her an unspeakable price. There was only one thing that could cause such aging in a young woman — he'd known in an instant that they had lost a child.

He couldn't get it out of his mind that if he'd stayed, Agnes might have lived. After all, Tom Estes would have provided the medicine needed. The master might be a hard man, but he wasn't cruel like Alice Leopold.

Agnes had been a sweet baby — docile and loving, always laughing. His firstborn. Howard had never realized his capacity to love until he set eyes on her ten years ago. And now she was gone forever.

Hannah couldn't mask the blame in her eyes when she'd looked at him. He'd seen it as clear as day, and it had cut him to the bone. Now he was asking her to take her remaining two children on a dangerous cross-country journey fraught with hazards. Howard didn't know if he was doing the right thing anymore.

The cemetery gate creaked on rusty hinges and the sound echoed in the hot night air. He pulled it shut behind him, and dug deep for the energy to keep walking toward Agnes' grave. Past the ornate headstones behind the fence that marked the graves of Clay County's white citizens he trudged, to the far corner of the cemetery where the Negro slaves had been interred for as long as he could remember.

It didn't take long for him to locate his daughter's grave. It was marked by a simple whitewashed cross, distinct from the others by its newness. He bent and traced the letters on the cross, recognizing his daughter's name:

Agnes Estes
1840 – 1850
Safe in the arms of Jesus

He sank to his knees on the dry, hard ground and bowed his head. "Agnes," he whispered, "Agnes. May God forgive me."

Howard knew God would forgive him, but could he forgive himself?

PROGRESS:

Forward or onward movement towards a destination;
advance or development towards completion or
betterment.

CHAPTER SEVEN

*I*t broke Momma's heart to leave Agnes behind in the cold, dry ground. She tried hard to hide it, but heartache shows up in the eyes. On the day she left Clay County, Momma's eyes were deep pools of pain.

The family went to say goodbye to Agnes together. The cemetery lay on a small rise just north of town. A wrought iron fence taller than Jenny separated the living from the dead. It was a cloudless, hot day, the air oppressive and heavy. As soon as she entered the cemetery, Jenny sat down under a tall black locust tree near her sister's grave and inhaled the honey-scented blossoms that hung in clusters above her head. She blinked back tears. A year had gone by since Agnes' death; Jenny missed her terribly.

She watched while Joseph and Daddy reinforced the wooden cross that marked her sister's final resting place. They added a fresh coat of whitewash to the weathered wood. When Jenny had cooled down, she picked a fresh bunch of wild yellow primroses and laid them over the grave. "Agnes will like these,"

Jenny said to Momma, reaching for her hand, but Momma gently pushed her away.

The family stood in a circle, heads bowed, around the grave and prayed for Agnes' eternal life. Then Daddy motioned to Jenny and Joseph. "Let's leave your Momma alone with Agnes for a few minutes," he said, his voice breaking.

Jenny laid her precious doll on the grave. "Goodbye, Agnes" she whispered.

She didn't want to leave her mother's side, but she reluctantly followed her daddy and her brother out of the graveyard. When they reached the gate, the path forked. The right path led to the road, the left to the area where the white people were buried. Her eyes brushed over the hand-painted sign identical to signs all over town: *No Coloreds.* Even people who couldn't read knew the meaning of those two words.

She peered over the wrought-iron fence into the white peoples' graveyard. There, the grave markers were more elaborate — headstones instead of wooden crosses — and crypts for the wealthier families. She cast a final glance back at Agnes' grave. "I'll remember you," she promised.

"Come on, honey," said Daddy.

But Jenny still hesitated at the gate. She looked back again to where Momma knelt on the ground, her body bent, her tears disappearing into the dry earth. Jenny wanted to run back to her mother and throw her arms around her, but Daddy took her hand firmly in his. "Leave her be, Jenny," he said. "This is between your momma and the Lord."

The family set off the next morning, traveling three weeks

ahead of Tom Estes and the herd of cattle. Not even Momma's grief could dampen Jenny's spirits as they left Clay County behind them. Mr. Leopold and Anna were there to see them off, but Mrs. Leopold stayed inside the house with her other children. Before they left, Mr. Leopold handed Daddy a bag. "You'll find some food and drink in here, in case you get hungry mid-morning," he said.

"We're grateful, Mr. Leopold," said Daddy, but Jenny knew that Daddy still held the Leopolds accountable for Agnes' death, and he was just being polite.

Finally they were on their way to freedom! Harriet Ross must have felt this same joy when she first set out, Jenny thought. Best of all, Daddy had been given the job of outfitting the wagon train, and Jenny was to be his right-hand helper.

The trip from Clay County Missouri, to Independence, Missouri was uneventful. Sometimes Jenny and Joseph walked along beside the wagon and sometimes they sat up behind their parents and listened to their conversation. Daddy was always optimistic about the future, but Momma didn't have much faith in things turning out well. One morning, Jenny overheard them talking: "We are heading straight into danger, thanks to the passing of the Fugitive Slave Act. What was Congress thinking?" Momma said.

"What's that?" piped up Jenny.

"It means that escaped slaves can be captured and brought back to their masters. It means an explosion in the business of slave catching," explained Daddy.

"But we're free now," Joseph protested. "We didn't escape.

We bought our freedom."

"That's no matter," said Momma. "It's our word against theirs. Whether you're a free man or an escaped slave, you can still be captured and returned to the south. The act states that our people have no right to a trial. In other words, we can't defend ourselves."

"I don't understand it," said Daddy. "They've made slave trading illegal up in Washington, but it's still legal to own a slave. For every step forward, it seems we take two steps back."

"Don't look for sense in everything," Momma said. "Life is not fair."

Jenny tried to ignore the bitterness that had crept into her momma's tone ever since they had left Agnes behind.

"Baby steps," said Daddy. "Things happen slowly. Progress walks softly and sneaks into our lives without us even noticing it."

CHOLERA:

An acute infectious disease of the small intestine, characterized by profuse watery diarrhea, vomiting, muscle cramps, severe dehydration and depletion of electrolytes.

CHAPTER EIGHT

$\mathcal{J}$enny knew that the town of Independence in Missouri sat at the head of the Oregon Trail. "Oregon," Jenny informed her daddy on their first evening in town, "became a territory less than a year ago. Mr. Estes told me that California hasn't joined the United States, but they will one day."

"Independence never sleeps," sighed Momma. "There's a lot of sin in this town."

Nobody could argue with her. At night, the men packed saloons, and from her family's campsite on Liberty Street on the edge of town, Jenny heard shouts and gunfire all night long. The local funeral director was quickly becoming a wealthy man, but it was cholera, not outlaws, that provided him with a steady flow of bodies. Filthy living conditions, dirty water and open sewage meant the disease spread easily amongst the pioneers. People died on the edge of their dreams and Jenny knew Momma had been right when she'd said that life isn't always fair.

In daylight, the streets were jammed with people of all ages and all colors. For the first time, Jenny saw free blacks —

successful business people such as store owners, wagon makers, blacksmiths, even gunsmiths. These were the men who would help them outfit their wagon train in the weeks to come.

Joseph walked around for the first three days with his mouth wide open and no words coming out of it. Momma stuck close to Daddy's side, impatient to leave Independence, while Jenny revelled in the new sights — the cowboys, the saloon girls, the merchants, the tradesmen, the constant noise and the ever-present dust.

This is almost as good as being a boy, she thought to herself. *No small children to look after, no mistress to obey. If this is what freedom is all about, then it suits me fine.*

The Prairie Traveler — A Handbook for Overland Travelers, was Jenny's constant companion. It had everything in it an overlander needed to know, and it was her job to create lists for Daddy so that he and Joseph could purchase their supplies with the money Tom Estes had given them.

"Here is a list of the clothes for one man, Momma: two red, or blue, front button flannel over-shirts …"

"I don't see why the color matters," Momma interrupted.

"Two wool undershirts, two pairs of stout shoes for walking, one pair of boots and shoes for horsemen, three towels, one poncho, one broad-brimmed hat of soft felt, one comb and brush, two toothbrushes, one pound castile soap, three pounds of bar soap for laundry, one belt knife and a small whetstone, one coat and one overcoat, stout linen thread, large needles, beeswax, a few buttons, a paper of pins and a thimble with all the sewing products in a small cloth bag."

By the time Tom Estes and his boys rode into Independence two weeks later, most of the provisions were purchased. Jenny had spent nearly a month perched up on the hard wagon bench, or trailing behind Daddy, the long list of necessary supplies spread open on her knee. Daddy couldn't have done it all without her — he'd said so dozens of times. She'd started with one long column of all the things she thought they'd need for the overland trip, and it had rapidly grown to three. As they acquired each item, Jenny put a neat tick beside it. Now, two weeks later, they had everything they'd need for the dangerous overland journey, plus an extra one thousand dollars in cash. It had cost just under six hundred dollars to outfit each wagon — more money than she'd ever seen before. Caravanning with Tom Estes had saved Jenny's family a lot of money and ensured the trip would be more comfortable than if they'd attempted it on their own.

A couple of days before the entire caravan was due to leave for the Oregon Trail, Jenny ran her eye down the list once more, hoping she'd left nothing out.

600 lbs flour
10 lbs rice
120 lbs biscuits
1 bushel dried fruit
400 lbs bacon
10 lbs cornmeal
60 lbs coffee
12 lbs ground corn

4 lbs tea (mostly for Momma)
keg vinegar
100 lbs sugar
3 gallons pickles
200 lbs lard
saleratus (baking powder)
200 lbs beans
8 lbs pepper
40 lbs salt

There was also 1 keg whiskey for medicinal and sipping — although Momma didn't think that was necessary at all.

In addition to all the food were the tools and equipment they'd need:

1 rifle
3 - 4 oxbows
2 pistols
5 lbs powder
10 lbs shot
mallet
wrench
tools
ox shoes
blacksmith tools
wagon tongues
wheels

grease (for the wagon wheels, to be applied once a day)
rope
spade
saw
axe
matches
cooking utensils
coffee pot
water and milk buckets
churn
kettle
tin plates and cups
65 lbs candles and soap (made by Momma)
60 lbs bedding
Ten pound sewing kit (from home)
clothing
washboard
Bible

Jenny and Daddy debated each of their purchases and shopped around for the best price. Tom Estes had put them in charge of outfitting all five wagons, so Jenny had to calculate every item recommended in the *Handbook* times the number of people traveling, and then check to see what each man already owned. She finally was able to use the arithmetic skills she'd learned in the Leopold household.

Daddy listened to all of Jenny's opinions and she felt a wave of pride when she overheard him bragging about the money she'd saved them. She also delighted in telling him facts about the journey ahead. "It's two thousand miles across the American Desert to California," she said. Or: "I heard there are over forty million buffalo on the prairie and when they move it sounds like thunder rolling across the ground."

"Is that right, girl?" Daddy would reply. "That's something!"

Their first big purchase had been two yoke of oxen for each wagon. Joseph thought they should buy horses, but Jenny said they were too expensive, and Daddy said the Indians would steal a horse at the drop of a hat.

"They don't take to oxen, though," he said, "and if we get hungry enough, we can eat them ourselves."

"But they're impossible to shoe," Joseph argued. "It will delay our start by two, maybe even three days."

It was true. The oxen had to be turned upside down to put the iron shoes on their feet and it took four men, instead of one for a horse. Still, Jenny felt the advantages outweighed the disadvantages. "Oxen are stronger and more even-tempered and Daddy says they take to the prairie grass better than a horse."

"You can't ride an ox," argued Joseph. "And they move at about two miles per hour."

In the end, the problem was solved when Tom Estes provided Joseph with a saddle horse of his own. "You can ride with the herd," he said.

Momma hadn't liked that idea at all. "What about Indians, or robbers, or a stampede?" she'd worried.

"I've got my pistol," said Joseph proudly.

After that, Momma and Daddy had words, and Joseph never mentioned his pistol again in front of Momma.

Tom Estes stood up for Joseph. "I could use an extra hand. We're a big group, ten teams. The boy doesn't want to ride in the wagons with the women. Oxen are the best choice for the wagons, but a boy that age is happier on a horse. Besides, no one will be foolish enough to attack such a large group, and the livestock will be too tired to walk after a week, let alone stampede. Let the boy ride with the men."

Finally, the day came to leave Independence.

They set off on April 6, 1851. It was a clear, warm day. A light breeze blew off the Missouri River, offering a brief respite from the mosquitoes that plagued Independence. Because it was early summer and thousands of migrants were heading west, the trail was crowded, forcing the Estes' wagon train to wait their turn behind other outfits.

People lined the street waving and wishing them good luck, just as Jenny and Joseph had done for other caravans every morning for the past few weeks. The migrants sang as they left Independence, their strong voices accompanied by the bawling cattle and the creaking and rumbling of the hundreds of wagon wheels rolling over the deeply rutted road.

The Estes' wagons sat low and heavy, loaded down with six tons of food and supplies for the six-month, two-thousand-mile trip. There were five wagons in the caravan altogether — three men per wagon plus the Estes family. Tom Estes, his two sons, Joseph, Daddy and the hands rode saddle horses, leading the train out of town. They made quite a parade as they wound their way through the crowded, dusty streets of Independence toward the first station on the trail, Fort Pillar.

Once on the prairie, the wagons rolled ahead of the herd. Even though the dust wasn't bad in Missouri, Daddy said it would get worse as the trail dried up, and if you got caught behind the herd you couldn't breathe, even with a handkerchief to cover your nose and mouth. Momma and Jenny rode together in the middle of the train because Momma was still nervous about driving the team — nervous, yet relieved to leave the swollen town in her wake.

Leaving Independence made Momma almost happy again. She'd hated the gunfights and the drinking, but the thing she feared most was the random, invisible killer: cholera. People were dying by the hundreds. The thought of losing one more of her children to disease had brought the familiar terror back into her heart. Now, westward bound, with the sun at her back and her future stretching out before her like her shadow across the prairie, she felt a renewed sense of hope. It seemed a new life might just be possible.

CONESTOGA:

Also called a Prairie Schooner; used by the United States pioneers to cross the prairies; a large wagon with broad wheels and an arched canvas top.

CHAPTER NINE

*J*enny skipped along the grassy verge beside the wagon. A handkerchief pressed to her nose did little to ward off the trail grit raised by the turning wheels of the hundreds of Conestoga wagons that snaked across the prairie like a moving city. She blinked constantly to clear the dust from her eyes, but it did no good. Her eyes stung and the afternoon heat drained her energy, but she felt happy.

Jenny kept her eyes to the ground, careful not to trip in the wheel ruts that grew deeper after every rainfall. A sprained ankle would mean hours spent under the cover of the Conestoga. On days when she tired of walking, she crept inside and curled up on the hard mattress to read or write in her journal, but she found the heat and the smell of canvas oppressive.

Daddy was right, thought Jenny: You can't rush progress. Every step toward the west might be a step toward freedom, but the train moved at a snail's pace.

Up in the wagon, sitting prim and upright as if the hard jockey bench were the most comfortable seat in the world,

Momma sang in a strong, deep voice. The lyrics in her songs reflected the experiences of the overland migrants:

> "I heard the tread of pioneers
> Of cities yet to be
> The first low wash of waves
> That soon shall roll a human sea."

Today had dawned hot and dry, and sunlight filtered through the throng of mosquitoes that darkened the sky. Jenny swatted at them unconsciously. She felt sorry for the livestock. If anything were going to drive them crazy, it would not be thirst, hunger or exhaustion, but the buzzing swarm of bloodsuckers that hung over them in a living, breathing cloud.

Everyone looked forward to the rain, but when it came, they all wished it away. Sometimes wheels sank so deep in the mud, it seemed as if the earth were reaching up and pulling them into the netherworld. When that happened, the men would hitch up extra oxen to the wagons and drag the wheels out of the quagmire.

Suddenly, off to the south, the sound of thousands of buffalo stampeding shook the earth beneath Jenny's feet. Gunfire filled the air. Jenny hated the buffalo hunt, hated the way the older animals circled the younger ones as if they could protect their calves from lead shot and bloodthirsty men. She hated the killing, but she loved the taste of fresh buffalo steak after a long day on the trail, and there were many nights when she was thankful for the thick buffalo skins that kept the cold away.

People said the Indians thanked the spirits of the animals they hunted down and killed. Jenny thought this was a fine idea, but it was one she kept to herself. Momma would say it was heresy to even contemplate that a dumb beast could have a soul.

After the hunt, the carcasses of the magnificent hump-backed animals that roamed the plains in the hundreds of thousands littered the sides of the trail, and their blood turned the hard dirt-brown ground an angry red. Some of the buffalo were left to rot where they fell with only their skins removed, their exposed bodies bloated and blue in the stifling heat. The stench of death rose off their decaying corpses, fouling the air. That combined with the clouds of flies buzzing around the bodies made Jenny's stomach turn.

In spite of all these hardships, Jenny's spirits remained high. She didn't miss Anna or her old life at the Leopolds. She tucked the memories of those days as a slave far away in the recesses of her mind.

"I'm free now," she whispered to herself, only half believing it and afraid to give full voice to the incredible truth.

Daddy felt the same way — she could tell by the light in his eyes and the fine laughter lines around his mouth. Even Momma seemed, if not happy, content. Jenny rarely saw Joseph except at mealtimes, where he entertained her with his stories about riding with the herd and the cowboys who were his trail companions.

They'd pushed hard the first three weeks out of Missouri. Tom Estes wanted to outride the cholera epidemic that was devastating Independence. Daddy and Momma and the rest of the men agreed with him. Momma prayed every morning and every night that the Good Lord would spare her family another death from illness. Jenny supposed He must have been listening, because everybody in their train had stayed healthy, except for bug bites, horse-kicks and a few bruises and cuts.

They'd passed through the territories of the Plains Indians — Pawnee, Cheyenne, Blackfoot and Apache — and although they'd heard many stories of massacres and robberies, they'd been left alone. In fact, as far as Jenny could tell, the Indians were to be more pitied than feared. Mostly they looked like hungry wanderers, not the warriors she'd heard tell of.

As well, the Indians were always willing to trade — fresh fish, skins or meat for pots or utensils or lead shot. In the beginning, Momma wouldn't go near them, but after a few days out, she realized that she was unlikely to be harmed. Eventually, she looked forward to their encampments. She said the Indians had wonderful fresh food, and she was always learning new recipes from the Indian women. Momma made Jenny stay in the wagon, hidden away. "Indians are unpredictable," Momma said. "They've been known to kidnap settlers' women and claim them as their own."

Jenny had met a few white men with Indian women on the trail, but she'd never seen an Indian man with a white woman, so she didn't know what to believe. It didn't matter, though — in the end, Momma's rules were the law.

The cattle and wranglers traveled two to three hours behind the train so that by the time they arrived at camp, the wagons were set up in a protective circle and Momma and Jenny had the meal well on its way. Because the trail was so crowded, Tom Estes had decided that they would do most of their traveling at night, whenever possible. Of course, the river crossings were all done in daylight because they were so dangerous. At the Platte River crossing, one of the wagons tipped over midstream and the caravan was delayed three days as everyone gathered the scattered contents and rested the tired oxen.

Wood was scarce, and it was Jenny's job to collect buffalo chips (and there were plenty) for the cook-fire. It wasn't much fun picking up buffalo dung, but it burned fast, clean and hot and didn't smell at all. Daddy said that they were making good progress traveling between sixteen and twenty miles a day, but that the pace would slow down once they reached the Rocky Mountains.

Occasionally they passed tattered wagon trains heading in the opposite direction, or small groups of stragglers shuffling along the trail on foot toward the east. These men, women and children would step aside and let the Estes wagon train roll past them. Jenny and her momma learned early on to avoid any form of contact or conversation with these people. They walked slowly, heads down, shoulders slumped, their eyes betraying the defeat they'd met somewhere along the trail.

The litter on the trail told their stories: broken wagons, damaged wheels and abandoned goods, including many hundred-pound sacks of precious bacon rotting in the sun. Sometimes, when wagons broke and the migrants ran out of parts, or when the oxen died, the trains had to double up and leave behind the supplies they couldn't carry with them. As well, crudely made crosses marked the hundreds of shallow gravesites where victims of disease, accidents and fights lay buried. Jenny could see that some of those people they passed heading back to Independence were traveling under the weight of broken dreams.

Fortunately, Daddy and Mr. Estes were familiar with the overland route, so they knew the best places to camp and graze the cattle, oxen and horses. Jenny, Momma and Joseph got used to drinking out of streams littered with sun-bleached animal bones. They also got used to the haunting cry of coyotes or wolves in the dead of the night — scavengers lurking in the shadows to pick off the weak or dying livestock. "We should shoot them, put them out of their misery," Jenny argued to her father. "You leave them on the trail and they get eaten alive."

"Lead shot is too expensive and if we run out, we can't replace it. I'm sorry, Jenny, but trail life is hard."

On June 16, just over two months out of Missouri, the train crossed the plains to Fort Laramie. The Estes caravan stayed in Fort Laramie for two days, enough time to replenish their dwindling supplies.

A little while earlier, Jenny had started a daily journal where she wrote down how many miles they'd covered and any problems encountered. On June 24, five days after the caravan had passed through Fort Laramie, she wrote:

Covered twenty miles today. We've already lost a number of cattle and three oxen, but Mr. Estes expected this. Camped eight miles west of Independence Rock. I wanted to climb to the top, but Momma wouldn't let me, even though Joseph was allowed. Not fair! Shoshone Territory.

Three days later, the caravan entered South Pass. Daddy called it the "Great Divide" and said their journey was halfway over. Jenny knew they must be high up, even though the trail ascended gently, because when she woke up in the morning there was ice as thick as a dinner plate and it covered everything.

They'd left the United States behind and were now in Oregon territory. Here, the Estes train veered southwest off the Oregon Trail toward California and freedom.

July 5, wrote Jenny. *Long, long day, but we only covered eighteen miles. We arrived at Parting of the Ways, five hours ahead of the herd. Mr. Estes chose the Sublette Cutoff because it will save us fifty miles. Everyone impatient.*

July 8. Waited three days to cross the Green River. Enjoyed the rest and washing off in the water. It was the scariest crossing yet. A rope with pulleys on it was stretched across the river, and a raft carried our supplies across. The raft held one wagon only and the current was very strong as we were going against it broadside. When we were nearly across, the upper edge of the boat went under water … and I thought the wagon would roll right off the end. Lucky it didn't, but I was scared. Momma prayed the whole way across.

August 11, Jenny wrote. *Fine, sunny morning. We left Ashlie Creek three miles back and passed over a long hill into the Bear Valley to Mineral Springs. There was a trading shanty and twenty*

or so Indian Wigwams. Soda Springs are a great mystery — six
feet deep and equally as wide. The water is hot, and smelly and
not fit to bathe in.

By the end of August, they'd been on the trail for almost six months. By the time they entered the Sacramento Valley, they'd lost over a third of their cattle and replaced half of their teams, but the Estes group remained intact. The closer Jenny's family got to Placerville, California, the mining town Daddy had chosen to be their home, the more their tired spirits soared. Placerville was sixty miles outside of Sacramento.

During the entire journey, the men had slept with rifles ready, taking turns on guard duty. The many crosses dotting the trail spoke of the dangers faced by all. As they finally neared Placerville, Jenny knew the hardships were almost over for her and her family.

"What a terrible thing to die so close to the end," Jenny thought when she passed the windswept graves only days away from their destination. To come this far and to fail seemed a cruel twist of fate. Jenny never missed the chance to place wildflowers on the mounds of earth just off the trail. It was the children's burial sites that caused her the most pain, because it reminded her of her sister way back in Clay County, Missouri.

Once over the Rockies, the migrants started to see a new kind of traffic on the road — wagons weighed down by tons and tons of flattened buffalo hides on their way to markets in California. Jenny had seen the skinned bodies of many of these magnificent animals on the trail, but had never understood where the pelts were going, or why the meat was left to rot beside the trail. Good thing there were more buffalo than people, she thought, because if it were the other way around, the hunters might run out of animals to kill.

By the time Jenny's family rolled into Placerville, all of them shared Daddy's dream of freedom. There had been plenty of black people on the Oregon Trail — people who had real jobs and got paid for their skills. People white men looked in the eye and treated like equals.

Still, despite the excitement, Jenny worried about Momma. She didn't seem herself. Every night she fell into bed exhausted. Daddy seemed not to notice. Finally, Jenny decided to speak to him. "Momma's ill," she said. She started to cry, because she knew that sick people usually go to heaven, and she didn't want Momma to leave her. "I heard her throw up when she thought she was alone."

"Honey," Daddy smiled and pulled her into his large arms. "Your Momma is just fine. She's not sick at all. She's carrying a new life inside of her."

"You mean …?"

"Your momma is going to have a baby — the first Estes to be born free!"

GOLD RUSH:

A rush to newly discovered goldfields in pursuit of riches.

CHAPTER TEN

A couple of days later, Momma and Jenny stood in the doorway of a cabin and surveyed their first real home. It was small, but there would be enough room for all of them. There was no glass in the windows and a thick layer of dust had settled on every surface. Still, Jenny could hardly believe it was theirs for the taking. *A home of their own.*

Daddy had explained that in Placerville people came and went and an empty cabin belonged to the first person to claim it — it was an unspoken law of the west. Miners stayed long enough to make their fortunes or to leave their shattered dreams behind them. The Gold Rush of 1849 had drawn thousands of gold seekers to California and now there was talk of the territory becoming part of the United States. But miners were not a settled folk. They didn't like to stay too long in one place.

"Our people are different," Daddy said. "We're looking for a home. Freedom is our fortune, not gold."

He was right. Although some blacks had the gold fever,

Jenny could see that most put their future in businesses — stores, blacksmiths' shops, barbers and grocers.

A few minutes passed and then Momma shifted uncomfortably. "Is the baby moving yet?" Jenny asked.

"If it is, I can't feel it yet," Momma laughed.

Jenny smiled and rested her head against her mother's tummy. Momma was almost two months into her pregnancy, and Jenny prayed the next seven months would pass quickly. "I can't wait until he's born," she said.

"He or she," Momma replied.

"I have a feeling it's a boy," said Jenny.

"Boy or girl," Momma smiled. "The Lord works in mysterious ways. We lost poor Agnes in slavery, and now this little one will be born into freedom. It's not a life for a life; I know things don't work that way, but I feel blessed to be bringing another baby into, I hope, a better world."

"It will be, Momma. It will," Jenny assured her.

Jenny felt a strange elation as she looked inside the crude cabin even though the family had little left after the overland trip. They were tired and grimy from the arduous trek into the new territories, but Daddy assured her that there was plenty of work in the mines.

Momma and Jenny went to work cleaning the cabin immediately. Neither of them minded the hard work. They'd never known anything else. And for the first time in their lives, they were working for themselves, not for somebody else.

They got to work quickly with bucket, soap, water, rags and mop, and within hours the cabin was as clean as could be expected. It was a small space of only three rooms, but they were a small family used to sleeping in close quarters. For the first time, they would live together as a family, seven days a week, not just on Saturdays and Sundays.

While her mother rested after cleaning, Jenny scavenged around the outskirts of Placerville until she found enough twigs for the fire. Wood was generally scarce near the town, but the gentle slopes of the Sacramento valley were covered in trees.

"I don't mind getting fuel," she said, "as long as I don't ever have to pick up another buffalo chip again."

Daddy returned home that first evening with a whole ham he'd bought for a dollar and a Dutch oven to cook it in. The ovens that had hung off the cook wagon belonged to Tom Estes, as had many of the cooking utensils, but finding new ones in Placerville proved a simple task. The miners left everything behind when they pulled up their stakes, including pots and pans, plates, knives, forks, spoons and cups. It seemed a terrible waste to Momma, but so did the way they lived their lives — they were dream chasers with no roots.

"Ungodly bunch," was how Momma described the loose band of men, and the women who lived off something Jenny didn't really understand — "the avails of prostitution."

Daddy began work in the gold mines three days after they'd arrived in the shantytown. And it wasn't long before both Jenny and Joseph were bringing in a whole dollar a day by panning for gold dust in the mountain streams. Momma decided to take in the white folks' laundry, even though her pregnancy had slowed her down quite a bit. It seemed everyone wore white, and there was no shortage of work. The miners wore pleated shirts and she charged them three dollars to wash and iron them. The frilly white dresses the women wore were even more difficult to launder, and for those, she charged five dollars a piece.

As Momma's pregnancy progressed, Jenny helped with the heavy loads of soiled clothing, and soon they'd made enough money to buy three chickens and a rooster. Any eggs they didn't eat themselves, they sold to the other homesteaders.

Food was expensive in California. Wheat flour cost fifteen dollars a barrel, so Momma instructed Joseph and Jenny to collect acorns, which she ground into her own flour. The children hunted the big grey squirrels that inhabited the hills outside of Placerville and learned to cook them the way the Indians did. First they pounded them, then they roasted them over an open fire, eating them bones and all.

At the end of each day, the family would place the money they'd earned in the middle of the wooden table and count it out carefully. Whatever they didn't need immediately would be hidden away in the tin can underneath Daddy and Momma's bed. Soon they had enough savings to buy a horse and wagon.

"We'll need one to get to San Francisco," Daddy said, and that was the first hint Jenny had that they wouldn't be staying forever in their new home. Nonetheless, Jenny turned eight and Joseph turned ten in the free state of California.

Sometimes Jenny felt guilty because she knew Momma and Daddy were working their fingers to the bone so that they could save up enough money to send her and Joseph to school. Daddy put a lot of store in education and he always said that he hadn't brought his whole family out to freedom so that they could live the lives of the ignorant.

School might have to wait for a year, but Momma insisted that they worship every Sunday. It wasn't difficult to find a Methodist church that accepted blacks and whites together. Jenny loved the new church in a way she'd never thought possible. The pious teachings of the men of God she'd known in Clay County were replaced by the loud, exuberant gospel stories and songs of the Methodist reverend who held service every Sunday morning at nine a.m.

Baby Booker was born May 9, 1852, seven months after the Estes family had settled in Placerville. He was a happy, robust little bundle who, Daddy liked to say, was "the first Estes born into freedom."

The birth was a difficult one for Momma, and her recovery period took them well into the next year. When Daddy deemed her strong enough to travel, the family packed up all their belongings, left behind the cabin at Placerville and moved to San Francisco.

"It's time for Jenny to go to school," Daddy said.

NEGRO:

A member of the black or dark-skinned group of human populations that exist or originated in Africa south of the Sahara, now distributed around the world.

CHAPTER ELEVEN

A little over a year later, Jenny sat across from her parents, twisting the material of her dress in her fingers.

"Stop fussing, Jenny," said Momma. "It does nothing to help this situation."

But Jenny couldn't stop fidgeting. She couldn't believe what her parents were telling her. She held the top marks for her grade, she never missed a day of school, and she'd won the spelling bee. In spite of this, the school superintendent insisted she couldn't stay in the all-white school she'd been attending for over a year.

"It's not fair. I'm smart," Jenny protested, "and I'm the best student they've got."

Booker, almost two years old, toddled over to her and tried to climb up onto her lap. Jenny pushed him away.

"Leave me alone," she said.

Booker burst into tears.

"Don't take it out on your brother," said Momma. "I don't know why everyone in this family is always expecting to be treated fairly when all we've ever been treated is unfairly. Do you think Agnes was treated fairly?" Her voice broke.

Daddy sighed. He put his hand on Momma's knee, but he looked annoyed.

"Peter Lester argued that very point with the school board. His daughter is pale like you. He lost. The law states that anyone with even an eighth of black blood is a Negro, and therefore must attend a segregated school. It looks like we don't have any choice in the matter," he said. He looked pointedly at his wife. "And things are only going to get worse here in the state of California."

"Jenny doesn't have to be in a white school to get an education," Momma retorted. "You've always put too much stock in her skin color. I knew it would only lead to disappointment in the end. Both of you forget that her even attending school is a gift we'd never have dreamed of when she was born."

Something in Momma's voice set off an alarm in Jenny. She glanced over at Daddy, who shrugged. His lips were set in a firm line and he stood up. Jenny didn't like this new, impatient side of Daddy.

"Hannah, things are changing rapidly in California. It's a free state only by name. There's talk of a head tax and of forcing us to wear identity badges. We can't vote, we can't testify in court and now our kids can't go to the schools of our choice. The Fugitive Slave Act means any one of us can be kidnapped off the street and returned to the south. Joseph has been beat up twice by white boys, and some people say the Ku Klux Klan has a chapter right here in San Francisco. I just wish you'd listen to some of the others. We're meeting every Monday night at the Zion Church. Why don't you come along? You'd be surprised at all the people you know and like who attend the meetings."

But Momma refused to attend the weekly meetings. "I know you're talking about leaving California," she said. "You promised me when we left Clay County that we wouldn't have to move again. I believed you. I won't even entertain the idea of leaving."

Momma was expecting another baby and this made her even more reluctant to move again. Just carrying the child seemed to sap her energy. More and more often, Jenny returned home from school to piles of laundry heaped on the kitchen floor and Momma asleep in her chair by the stove. On those days, Booker, hungry and bored, rushed into Jenny's arms. "Take me out to play," he'd beg.

Jenny would have liked nothing better. She longed to escape the cramped, heavy atmosphere in their cabin. There was always something to see in San Francisco, but she had to do Momma's work: cook dinner, deliver the clean laundry and do her homework on top of everything else. Often she didn't get to bed until well after midnight.

Only she and Booker were home seven months later when Momma's labor pains started. Daddy and Joseph were at the store they'd started with Daddy's good friend Peter Lester. The store's success meant Momma didn't have to work so hard and Jenny could concentrate more on her schoolwork — which is what she'd been doing when Momma called out to her to go and fetch Mahala Lester.

Jenny left a puzzled three-year-old Booker at Momma's side and ran for the midwife, who lived only five minutes down the road. She burst through the front door without knocking. "The baby is coming," she panted. "The pains started in the night and Momma says they were mild, but suddenly they got really bad!"

Mrs. Lester put down the newspaper. "You gave me a real start," she said, "bursting through the front door like that. I was having a bit of a break. I just delivered Mrs. Clayton of an eight-pound baby girl. I was up all night with her. Calm yourself, Jenny. I'll get my things and be right there. You run ahead and stay with your Ma. Go on, now. And for goodness sake, stop worrying. Your momma has brought plenty of babies into the world."

Jenny didn't think that Mrs. Lester looked like a midwife, but she certainly acted the part. Midwives, Jenny thought, should be short, round and motherly women, not tall and beautiful like Mrs. Lester. Mrs. Lester instilled confidence wherever she went. She had delivered many babies in her time, but didn't have children of her own. She wasn't concerned about Momma because Momma had delivered five healthy babies, the first at sixteen.

She wasn't concerned, that is, until she stood beside Momma's bed ten minutes later, her hand on Momma's forehead. "You're burning up," she said.

"Something's not right, Mahala," Momma replied in a small voice. "I've known it for a long time."

Mrs. Lester touched her friend's extended stomach. She prodded and poked and the more she explored, the more thoughtful she became. "Please take Booker out of the room," she directed Jenny. "And then come right back. I'll need you."

Jenny planted Booker in the back yard. "Stay here and don't come in until I come and get you."

Inside, Mrs. Lester was talking to Momma. "How long have you had the pains?"

"Off and on through the night, but not bad, just little sharp jabs and lots of time between each one." Momma spoke slowly, each word an effort. " I sent Howard off to work this morning."

Jenny put her ear close to Momma's dry lips. Clearly it pained her to speak. A moist sheen of sweat bled through her unusually pale skin. She moaned.

"I tried to make her comfortable," Jenny told Mrs. Lester. She felt a prickle of fear that began in her tummy and slithered up to catch in her dry throat.

"You've done well." Mrs. Lester smiled, a smile that didn't reach her eyes. "Don't let her down now." She noted the makeshift curtain Jenny had drawn around the bed, the damp towels and the cup of water on the rough bedside table. "When did she last eat?"

"Yesterday, lunch. She had a taste of chicken soup." Jenny had spoon-fed her, sure that Momma only had a touch of the flu. Maybe she should have done more.

Mrs. Lester prodded Momma's tummy some more and then she sat on the edge of the bed. She took Momma's limp hand in hers. "Hannah, this baby doesn't want to come out. It's all turned around: its head where its feet should be and its feet where its head should be."

"Lord," breathed Mama. "My back hurts so bad." A single tear ran down her cheek.

"Jenny, take Booker to Jessie Franklin's place and leave him there. This might take some time. Tell her the baby is breech and I'm going to try to right it. After that run and get your daddy. Hurry now."

"Let me say goodbye to Booker," Momma breathed.

"Not goodbye," whispered Jenny. "Please, Momma, not goodbye."

"Get Booker, child." Momma squeezed Jenny's hand.

Jenny fetched Booker, but he was afraid to approach the bed. "Come here, baby," Momma said. He moved to her bed obediently and threw his arms around her neck. "I love you," Momma said. "You'll have to be brave, like your daddy and your brother and sister."

"Now Hannah …" began Mrs. Lester.

"Mahala, don't deny me saying goodbye. Just in case. You can't fault me for that."

Thirty-six hours later, Eliza arrived. Eliza, blue and screaming. Eliza, dark haired, dark skinned and angry.

Mrs. Lester pushed the baby into Daddy's arms. "You tend her," she instructed him, "she's strong and healthy in spite of everything. Jenny, help me change the bed, then we'll clean your mother up. I've got to stem the bleeding." Mrs. Lester's voice trembled.

Jenny did as she was told, her limbs moving automatically. So much blood.

In her thoughts, she was back in Clay County. Back with Agnes.

And Agnes had died in spite of all their efforts.

They were all busy. Joseph kept the stove stoked. Jenny

followed Mrs. Lester's instructions. Daddy sat and held Momma's hand. Momma lay perfectly still.

She couldn't feed the baby.

Mrs. Lester sent Joseph to milk the nanny goat. "Goat's milk won't harm the child," she said.

Jenny didn't care about *the child,* but she kept her peace. Momma's skin grew paler as her life drained out of her, pooling in a puddle of blood on the sheets. Jenny held a damp cloth to Momma's cracked lips. "Dear, sweet Jesus," she prayed silently, "let her live."

Eliza, the cause of all this chaos, sucked hungrily on a milk-drenched cloth. She clenched her tiny fists and screamed between feedings, before dropping off into short, fitful sleeps.

"She wants to see the baby," Mrs. Lester said, hours later.

Daddy held Eliza up for Momma to see. Joseph gripped his momma's arm, while Jenny stood silently at her head, her warm, shaky hands on Momma's cold skin.

Momma opened her eyes, too weak to move. "Eliza," she whispered. "Jenny, promise me you'll care for her, love her — and Booker too."

Jenny nodded. "I'll take care of them until you are better, Momma." She choked back a sob. "I promise you that."

Momma closed her eyes. "Agnes," she whispered. She smiled. Her chest rattled and stilled.

Daddy began to cry.

"Your momma has gone to join our Lord," Mrs. Lester said. "I do believe her Agnes met her at the Pearly Gates."

EMIGRATE:

To leave one's own country to settle in another.

CHAPTER TWELVE

The family buried Momma on the following Saturday. All of their neighbors and the people they'd become friends with in California attended. The service was held in the local church, but people came from as far away as Placerville. In the short time they'd lived there, the Estes had become liked and respected members of the community.

Jenny didn't remember a thing about that day, except that she wanted it to end.

Afterwards it took Jenny a long time to learn not to hate baby Eliza. But a promise was a promise, and looking after Eliza was the last thing her momma had asked her to do. So Jenny determined to do it, no matter how difficult.

Eliza, for her part, seemed completely unaware of the burden her life had brought to her family. She was a noisy, difficult baby, who slept only an hour at a time, and cried often. She demanded and got all of Jenny's attention. She slept in Jenny's bed at night, and in the daytime, when Jenny wasn't at school, Jenny carried her wherever she went. It was a blessing when Eliza fell asleep, but if Jenny tried to put her down, Eliza would wake up screaming.

It was as if Eliza knew she had no momma to love her. If she didn't draw attention to herself, everyone might just ignore her existence.

Mrs. Lester looked after Booker and Eliza when Jenny was at school. "It's the least I can do for your momma. She was a good woman and she wouldn't have wanted you to leave your studies. Besides, I don't have my own children and I enjoy their company."

Daddy did his best to love his new daughter as he loved Jenny, Joseph and Booker, but he found it difficult. "Every time I look at her, I see your momma," he told Jenny. "And I know it's wrong, but I can't help thinking that if it weren't for Eliza, she'd still be here."

Joseph made no attempt to hide his dislike of Eliza. He ignored her, acting as if the new baby didn't exist. Only Booker seemed to take pleasure in his baby sister. He laughed at her when she howled and pinched her when she was finally quiet — actions that earned him severe reprimands from Jenny and the rest of the family.

After Momma died, Daddy grew quieter and more determined to leave California. "There's nothing to keep us here now," he said sadly. "Nothing at all."

Jenny knew that Momma would have told him that happiness comes from inside a person, and didn't have much to do with where one lived. Momma would have told him to stop running. But Momma was gone, and Jenny wasn't sure how to put these thoughts into words.

Joseph changed after his mother died. He spoke only if spoken to and his normally subdued temper became sullen and uncooperative. He quit school halfway through the year and went to work in the store full-time. "I'm not much into book learning," he told Daddy. "I like being in the store."

Daddy wasn't too pleased about it, but he agreed. Business was booming and he could use extra help.

Only Booker and Eliza carried on as usual, at least on the outside. Booker missed Momma, but he didn't understand the permanence of death. Jenny determined to never let him forget their mother, and in the evenings, no matter how exhausted she was, she lay beside him in bed and whispered family stories in his ears. She didn't talk much about Agnes, although Jenny missed both her and Momma terribly. Her conversations about Agnes were short and to the point: "Our big sister Agnes died when she was ten going on eleven. She would have loved you. She's with Momma in heaven. She died in Clay County, Missouri."

"Why?" Booker always asked.

"She got sick," Jenny replied. But she wanted to say, "Because God is cruel."

So, at ten, Jenny Estes' childhood ended abruptly. Her momma's death catapulted her unwillingly into adulthood. Even though Mrs. Lester helped out and Jenny managed to attend the nearby Negro school most days, it fell to her to look after the younger children, to do the laundry and the house-work and feed Daddy and Joseph when they arrived home tired each evening after a long day at the store.

Late at night, after the children were asleep, she mended

clothes and listened to her father talk about his dreams for the future. He'd become more and more involved in politics after Momma died. He believed that one day all men might live equally in the United States of America, but he also thought that day was far away. "There'll be a war in this country before equality becomes a right," he told Jenny. "North against South. I'd rather bring up my children in peace."

As a black person, Daddy wasn't allowed to vote, but he and his friends were closely following the political progress of a man named Abraham Lincoln. "If Lincoln ever becomes the president," he said, "there will be hope for our people."

Secretly, Jenny doubted if anyone against slavery could be elected president — even a white man. If it ever happened, it would be a miracle.

Restless, lonely and missing her mother, Jenny slowly began to see the advantages of uprooting and starting all over again.

THE DRED SCOTT DECISION, 1857: "A free Negro of the African race, whose ancestors were brought to this country and sold as slaves, is not a 'citizen' within the meaning of the Constitution of the United States."

CHAPTER THIRTEEN

Three months after her momma died, Jenny started attending the Monday night meetings at the Church of Zion with Daddy and his friends. Racial tension between the Northern and Southern States was on the increase, and there was talk among black people of a mass exodus out of California — but to where, nobody knew.

"It doesn't matter where we go, as long as we can live in freedom and peace. The soul knows no borders," Daddy liked to say. Jenny agreed.

The meetings at the Church of Zion were not religious; they were political. The men and women talked about "The Fate of Our People." A new word began to filter into Jenny's vocabulary: *emancipation*. The conversations and debates reminded her of those held behind closed doors in Clay County when she was a little girl.

In early 1857, the United States Supreme Court ruled on the Dred Scott vs. Sandford case. Everyone in the Church of Zion, and all over America, awaited the court's decision.

Dred Scott was a black slave from Missouri who'd lived for seven years with his master in the free state of Illinois. This allowed him to apply for his freedom — which he did, but he was turned down. The Supreme Court judges ruled that people of African origin — free or enslaved — could never be and never had been U.S. citizens. Therefore, as non-citizens they didn't have the right to sue. In addition, the judges, who were wealthy southern slave owners, ruled that prohibiting slavery in free states was against the constitution. Scott lost. Americans, both black and white, were incensed and the great split began between north and south that would eventually lead to civil war.

The members of the Church of Zion received the Dred Scott decision with disbelief and shock. One day after the ruling, they called an emergency meeting.

In a sombre voice, Mifflin Gibbs summarized the Supreme Court's decision to the horrified parishioners: "African Americans cannot be Citizens of the United States," he said, his voice grave. "African Americans have no rights to Citizenship."

He paused and let the words sink in, before continuing. "Do you realize that even as we in the so-called Free State of California gather to plan our next moves, slave ships continue to sail into Alabama on a daily basis? There are only four thousand of us, and half a million white folks in this state, and yet they fear us. Times will only get worse. Oregon's new constitution forbids free black people from entering that state. We can either stay here and lose more of our hard-fought freedoms every hour, or go somewhere we are wanted."

Soon after that meeting, Daddy brought home a public notice

and placed it on the table in front of Jenny. "Read this to me, please," he asked, sitting down opposite her.

Jenny read the words aloud slowly:

> *There will be a public meeting of the colored citizens of San Francisco this (Friday) evening April 14, at Zion ME Church, Pacific, above Stockton St., to commence at 8 o'clock.*
>
> *Signed by a Committee.*

Jenny and her daddy already knew that the Church of Zion committee was studying where the community could move en masse. For months they'd had their eyes on Sonora, Mexico, but the discovery of gold up north had changed that. Suddenly, the English territories were opening up. Within days of the news of a rich strike in the Thompson River in 1858, thousands of gold-seekers began to flock to New Caledonia. Gold. It seemed to Jenny that the fate of her family was linked inextricably to the shiny, yellow metal that the ground coughed up every ten years or so.

On April 14, 1858, the air in the cramped church hummed with excitement. Everyone had turned out for the meeting. Jenny sat in the crowd, Eliza balanced on her knee, Booker pressed against her. Beside her, Joseph and Daddy waited impatiently for the meeting to begin. All eyes were riveted on the pulpit.

Riveted on a certain Captain Nagel.

The captain was nervous. He fixed his steel-blue eyes on the sea of black faces in front of him, than turned to the letter he held in his hand. "Ahem," he cleared his throat, and a hush fell over the church. Governor Douglas, who ruled over the land of

New Caledonia on behalf of the British Crown, was counting on him. If Captain Nagel failed to convince these people to go north, Governor Douglas would never trust him again.

Governor Douglas feared that his colony up north was at risk of being taken over by its aggressive southern neighbors. What better way to protect themselves than by importing nearly a thousand able-bodied men and women who would do anything, defend anything, in the name of their own freedom?

At first Captain Nagel had been doubtful about Sir Douglas' idea to invite a whole community of colored people to New Caledonia. There were rumors that the Governor himself came from a mixed-blood background, and maybe that explained why he'd seen value in these people when others hadn't. But now that he'd met some of them, Captain Nagel had to admit a grudging respect for these men and women.

He cleared his throat again, unfolded the letter with the official seal on the front and began to read:

"James Douglas, Governor of the Colony and head of the Hudson's Bay Company, welcomes all of you and promises that under the British flag you will be accepted on free and equal terms."

A huge cheer rose from the assembled crowd.

Captain Nagel stood quietly at the podium, waiting for the crowd to calm down. He'd been well-received, better than he'd dared hope. Mifflin Gibbs stepped forward and gestured to the crowd for silence. He held out his hand and clasped the captain's. "Welcome to San Francisco and the Church of Zion. Before you begin your presentation, our choir has prepared a song to honor your very generous invitation to our people."

He nodded to the choir, who stood in unison. Everyone in the audience clapped and called out encouragement. Jenny sat back, rocking Eliza gently, and let the words of the song wash over her.

> "Look and behold our sad despair
> Our hopes and prospects fled,
> The tyrant slavery entered here,
> And laid us all for dead.
>
> Sweet home! When shall we find a home?
> If the tyrant says that we must go
> The love of gain the reason,
> And if humanity dare say "no"
> Then they are tried for treason.
>
> God bless the Queen's majesty,
> Her scepter and her throne,
> She looked on us with sympathy,
> And offered us a home.
>
> For better breathe Canadian air,
> Where all are free and well,
> Then live in slavery's atmosphere
> And wear the chains of hell.
>
> Farewell to our native land,
> We must wave the parting hand,

Never to see thee any more,
But seek a foreign land.

Farewell to our true friends,
Who've suffered dungeon and death.
Who have a claim upon our gratitude
Whilst God shall lend us breath.

May God inspire your hearts,
A Marion raise your hands:
Never desert your principles
Until you've redeemed your land."

By the last stanza, there was not a still foot or a dry eye in the whole building. Captain Nagel was impressed with the knowledge these people already possessed about his country. He was thoroughly convinced that Governor Douglas' idea to make them British subjects had been ingenious.

Mifflin Gibbs stepped forward again. "Quiet, everyone," he said. "There will be plenty of time for questions."

Gibbs was a highly respected member of the San Francisco black community. He was a self-educated man who edited the newspaper they all depended on, *The Mirror of Our Times.* He'd been raised in Philadelphia and loved to tell stories of his days as a part of the Underground Railroad.

Jenny knew him well. He and Peter Lester and Daddy had been successful partners in a leather goods store for a couple of years, and Daddy trusted him. If Mr. Gibbs supported Captain Nagel's too-good-to-believe offer, then there must be something in it.

The captain held up a large, tattered map of New Caledonia. Jenny shifted forward with the whole congregation in one fluid movement. It was a magic map, a mysterious map: the map of their future.

She glanced over at Daddy. His eyes sparkled like they hadn't since Momma had died. They shone the same way they had just before the family fled Clay County, Missouri, to freedom. A shiver of apprehension or anticipation, she couldn't decide which, ran up her spine. In that moment, she knew for sure she would be leaving California forever.

Captain Nagel called himself a "British Subject." He looked American, but he spoke in a strange crisp manner, his words clipped and difficult to understand.

"I'd be pleased to field any questions you might have," he said, nervously clearing his throat. Jenny tried not to laugh when he spoke, but his accent was funny. He shortened his vowels, hardly bothered to pronounce his "H's" and peppered his sentences with words like "please" or "right," or "what ho." He talked as if he had a mouthful of sour lemon, but he sounded polite. Jenny knew Momma would have approved.

It seemed as if everyone in the Methodist church had something to ask Captain Nagel about New Caledonia. Jenny held Booker's hand and listened, praying that Eliza wouldn't misbehave and force her to leave in the middle of the meeting.

"What, sir, is the degree of latitude?" asked a man sitting near the front of the church.

"Fort Victoria lies just below the 49th parallel." Captain Nagel held up the map and pointed out the exact location of the territory. Jenny strained forward to look. She could just make out that New Caledonia lay north of Oregon Territory. It was a large island on the edge of the continent. Jenny's heart fluttered. Hadn't Momma always told her that there was no better life than island life? Visions of Madagascar filled her head.

"What is the population of Vancouver Island?" somebody else asked.

"The British in Fort Victoria number five hundred, and on the whole island, there are a thousand in total. Of course, there are the Indians and the half-breeds, but I don't know their numbers. So far they've given us little trouble."

"Is Fort Victoria a part of New Caledonia?" asked a man at the very back of the church.

"Fort Victoria is the capital of our Crown Colony," Captain Nagel said proudly.

"Is the Hudson's Bay Company the government?"

"No, the HBC is simply a trading outfit. The colony is governed by James Douglas and is protected under the British Flag."

"It seems to me that by the way Fort Victoria is positioned, the Americans might mistake it for their own territory and then where would we be?" Mr. Lester always asked the hard questions, the smart questions.

"On the side of the British," Captain Nagel replied shortly. There was a pause, then he continued: "We need you," he said. "The gold discovery means it is only a matter of time until the Fort is overrun with Americans. We need laborers and soldiers. And you need a home."

"Is there any truth to the rumors of gold being found on the Fraser River?"

"Right, well, at this point that has not been confirmed," Captain Nagel hedged. "However, what we are offering you is better than gold. We are offering you freedom."

A massive cheer went up, and the very sides of the building vibrated with joy.

"Hold on here a minute," shouted out a lone dissenter, struggling to make his voice heard over the clamor. "I don't like the sounds of this Hudson's Bay Company. They might not want others in competition against them. We're businessmen, shopkeepers and skilled laborers. Besides, it sounds like there's a short growing season on Vancouver Island."

The crowd booed. "Let him speak," one man shouted. "Everyone should have their say."

"Thank you," the dissenting man said. "What about the weather on Vancouver Island? It sounds like too harsh a climate to me. I think we should consider Sonora, Mexico."

"It's true that the weather is sometimes variable," Captain Nagel said. "We have our share of snow and cold, but the growing season is long and the soil is rich. Wildlife is abundant and the waters around Vancouver Island are teeming with sea life. Nobody goes hungry in New Caledonia."

Now Mifflin Gibbs took over again and the crowd hushed. "The debate about where we'll live should be held amongst our own people. We have a committee appointed just for that. Let's leave discussions and final decisions for another day. Captain Nagel is available for questioning for the next hour. For those of you who have to leave, I propose another meeting for the night of April 19."

Jenny, who'd been struggling with Eliza for the last ten minutes, gratefully stood up. She signalled to Daddy that she would be going home, grabbed hold of Booker and hurried out of the church into the warm San Francisco night.

On April 19, 1858, the community as a whole decided to accept Governor Douglas' generous offer and leave California for the north.

For the third time in her short life, Jenny found herself bound for a new home, this time without Momma to reassure her.

CROWN COLONY:
A colony controlled by a foreign monarchy, managed through an appointed governor.

CHAPTER FOURTEEN

wo months after the eventful town meeting with Captain Nagel, the *Commodore* sailed out of San Francisco carrying four hundred black Americans, including Jenny, Booker and Eliza. The journey from San Francisco to Fort Victoria would take four days.

Daddy and Joseph had already left overland, driving a small herd of their own cattle up the Oregon Trail to sell in Washington. Another four hundred black people would follow over the next two weeks.

The *Commodore*, which many had affectionately named the Freedom Ship, was a derelict old steamer, overcrowded and barely seaworthy. The wind picked up once they left the sheltered waters of San Francisco Bay and the livestock careened wildly in the hold as the waves lifted and tossed the ship. Jenny feared that they were at risk of capsizing. She became too seasick to look after Eliza and had to entrust her sister's care to six-year-old Booker.

On the second day, the weather worsened, although Jenny's seasickness abated enough that she was able to take the children above deck for some fresh air. There she saw a terrible sight that would haunt her for the rest of her life.

In order to lighten the ballast in the stormy seas, Captain Nagel reluctantly ordered forty horses to be thrown overboard. Jenny watched in horror as the helpless animals, frantic with terror, were forced over the side of the ship. They landed heavily in the rolling ocean and their screams filled the air. The *Commodore* ploughed mercilessly northward, leaving the animals to their watery graves.

Two or three white men, drunk on whiskey, raised their pistols and began target practice on the terrified animals. They laughed and talked as they shot.

"Come on, Booker," Jenny said, taking his hand firmly and lifting Eliza to her hip. She stumbled to the bow of the ship and vomited over the side.

Five days later, without any other incident, the ship docked in Fort Victoria. Passengers of every description disembarked: gold miners, thieves, outlaws, fortune hunters, good-time girls and adventurers. Only the black Americans fell on their knees and kissed the ground of their new homeland.

Overnight, Fort Victoria had been transformed from a small town with ten buildings and a population of a hundred people into a booming mining town. Two hundred and twenty-five buildings had sprung up in the muddy earth where earlier there had been five. And people still continued to pour into the coastal town. Every two days a steamer arrived from San Francisco, depositing fortune hunters, entrepreneurs and dreamers into New Caledonia.

It meant plenty of work for Daddy and Joseph — the family was finally able to start saving money again so they could buy their own land. But at five dollars an acre, property near Victoria was beyond their means.

"On the other hand, we can pre-empt land, good land, at only a dollar an acre a short distance across the water on Salt Spring Island," said Daddy.

"What's pre-empt?" Booker asked.

"It means we only have to pay the Crown, or the Government, a dollar an acre, and we don't have to hand over any money until the land is surveyed. We get four years to pay, which means the land should be earning its keep by then. As long as we live on and work the land, it's ours," Jenny explained patiently. "And we would still live on an island like Momma did when she was a little girl." Jenny could still hear her mother's voice: "Madagascar is the best place in the world. There is nothing better than island living."

"Salt Spring," said Daddy and again he looked to the future.

Jenny and Joseph recognized that old, familiar look in his eyes and they knew that Victoria would not be their home for long. The majority of their fellow-passengers on the Freedom Ship had opted to stay in or near Fort Victoria where they could build their businesses to support the burgeoning population. The English — true to their word — accepted the blacks in their churches and schools, but Jenny had noticed that the white Americans brought their dislikes with them to New Caledonia.

So it was that a little more than a year after arriving in Fort Victoria, Jenny stood on the bow of another ship: the schooner

Black Diamond. Her arms were wrapped around her body to protect herself from the cold winter wind. Her skirt billowed out around her thin legs and she shivered. In spite of the bright October sun, she felt the chill of the north in her bones. The dry heat of California seemed a lifetime away, and she worried, not for the first time, how she would cope with the long, inhospitable winters in this strange new land.

PRE-EMPTION:

The right of purchasing before others, given by the government to the actual settler upon a tract of public land; the purchase of something under this right.

CHAPTER FIFTEEN

The ship had been at anchor for only a few minutes. Vesuvius Bay, a small finger-shaped inlet on the northeast edge of Salt Spring Island, lay before Jenny. Behind her, the Saanich Peninsula extended lazily out into the murky-green Pacific Ocean. Somewhere beyond the peninsula, Jenny knew, was the bustling Fort Victoria they had left behind that very morning.

For a second, Jenny felt the familiar panic welling up inside of her. *I don't want to be here. I want to go home.* But this *was* her home now — this wild British colony called New Caledonia.

The sailing sloop shifted gently in the wind and Jenny gripped the railing tightly. She couldn't wait to get off the *Black Diamond* and onto firm ground. With a strong wind behind them, the trip across Sansum Narrows to Salt Spring Island had taken less than an hour. Fuelled by excitement, Eliza and Booker hadn't sat still for a second. Instead they'd done their best to get under the feet of the cattle or fall overboard. Jenny longed to be alone. She was tired of looking after the children.

It wasn't fair. Sometimes, when she thought about her momma, she felt angry. "I'm more of a slave now than I ever was," she would say to herself. Then she would ask the Lord for forgiveness. It was sinful to think ill of the dead and Momma hadn't wanted to die, hadn't intended to leave her with so much responsibility.

Salt Spring lay like a sleeping giant in cool fall sunshine. Jenny wondered about the people who would be her neighbors.

Thirty-three new settlers had taken advantage of the offer to pre-empt land on Salt Spring. None of the Australians were married. Daddy said these men couldn't afford wives, not after throwing their money after gold fields, booze and women — "empty promises for empty men" was how he put it.

There were a handful of Scots, a few Irish, even some Hawaiians, and of course the British, but the majority of the new settlers, seventeen of the twenty-nine, were naturalized blacks — families with children.

"No Americans to contend with, at least not yet," Daddy pointed out.

Just about everyone said that, but Jenny knew those hopeful words disguised a fear that one day their southern neighbors might decide to move to Salt Spring too. The Scots and the Brits and Aussies had strange accents and odd ways, but they didn't hate people because of their skin color.

At least not openly.

"Tuan," Jenny said softly. The Indian name for the island she would now call home rolled off her tongue easily. The English had tried to change its name to "Admiral Island," although most people referred to it as "Salt Spring" or "Tuan." She smiled to herself, because nobody called it Admiral, even though it was the official name on the maps she'd seen.

She stared up at the heavily treed slopes to where the cabin that Daddy had built awaited them. Daddy and Joseph had spent the summer on Salt Spring clearing the land, while she and the children stayed behind in Fort Victoria with the Lesters.

Daddy had told her that the Indians were friendly. "They're Coast Salish people from the Penelakut Indian village, not far from here on Kuper Island." They came at low tide to gather the clams that grew knee-deep in the quiet bays along the rocky, meandering shoreline. They hunted the wolves, cougars and deer that lived in the dense forest covering most of the island. Jenny wasn't scared of the Indians, but she didn't like the idea of sharing her home with so many wild animals.

A gull screeched overhead and Jenny started. Behind her, the last few cattle on board bawled restlessly, sliding and scrambling for footing on the slippery deck. They shifted from foot to foot as the *Black Diamond* rose and fell in the gentle sea. The men cursed as they struggled to lash the thick ropes around the quivering bodies of the terrified livestock.

Jenny watched for a minute, than turned away. Her stomach rolled and heaved. Cattle fear, like human fear, carries its own distinct smell. She closed her eyes and took a deep breath, than exhaled slowly so that the salty wind carried the rancid scent away from her and scattered it over the water.

Four of their fifteen cattle had already reached the shoreline, their struggle to find firm ground beneath their hooves over, while three others had crossed the beach and were headed off up the narrow trail leading to their cabin.

Seven-year-old Booker clutched Jenny's hand and Jenny balanced a sleepy four-year old Eliza on her hip until she was so uncomfortable she could no longer bear her sister's weight.

"Take Eliza for a while, Booker."

Booker took his little sister reluctantly. "Thanks," Jenny said, stretching her aching arms out in front of her. "Eliza is getting heavier by the minute."

She blinked rapidly, tears welling unexpectedly in her dark eyes. She turned her head so that Booker wouldn't see.

"Momma," she whispered, the word catching in her throat, but already it sounded unfamiliar, as if she no longer had any right to it.

Eliza squirmed in Booker's arms. She reached toward Jenny. "Ma," she said. "Ma."

"No," retorted Jenny, "I'm not Ma. I'm Jen. And I'm not going to take you, my arms are sore." She stepped back, out of sight of her sister. The effort it took to love Eliza hadn't lessened with time.

"I promise I'll take care of her, Momma, but you're asking a lot," Jenny said to herself.

According to Daddy, Momma was "at home with God." Jenny imagined her serious mother keeping company with a stern, long-bearded white man, the two of them perched on the edge of a fluffy cloud. The image made her laugh in spite of herself.

She missed Momma more, not less, every day, but she had

learned to hide her sadness from everyone else. Nonetheless, Jenny missed her momma first thing in the morning when she woke up and she missed her last thing at night, before she fell into exhausted sleep. All through the day, no matter what she did, she thought about Momma — but only a little, otherwise she couldn't continue sweeping the floor or milking the cows or cooking the dinner. Otherwise she would sit right down on the spot and cry a river of tears, greater even than the Mississippi.

During the first few weeks after Momma's death, she'd wept into the warm sides of the cows she milked and into the soapy laundry water and into the stew pot, but eventually she'd learned to cry inside.

Now, Jenny's big brown eyes fell onto Booker. He clutched the squirming Eliza tightly. "I have my freedom," she said to herself, "but I am more tied down than ever."

"What's the matter, Jenny?" Booker leaned into his oldest sister, concern in his wise, young eyes.

Nothing, Booker. Nothing at all.

Eliza wiggled, reaching out to Jenny at the sound of her voice.

"I was just thinking out loud." Jenny lied. "Give me Eliza, before you drop her overboard."

"You were thinking about Momma again," Booker accused her.

"Yes, perhaps, but I'm tired, too." She smiled reassuringly at Booker. He seemed so much older than his seven years. "Go and ask Mr. Macauley how long 'til we're off the ship. Be careful," she added, "and stay away from the cattle and the men."

Mr. Macauley was the local Hudson's Bay Agent. He traveled between the trading posts regularly, and now that settlers were moving to Salt Spring he made the journey across the strait once or twice a month, weather allowing. He knew all the sailors on the *Black Diamond*, and today he was in charge of seeing Jenny and her siblings safely across the narrows.

"He's got the bluest eyes I've ever seen," Booker had whispered to Jenny, when he first met Mr. Macauley at the dockyard in Victoria.

"You say that about every white person you meet," Jenny retorted.

"But I really mean it this time," Booker replied. "I can see the summer sky in his eyes."

Momma always said Booker would grow up to be a preacher or a poet, he had such a way with words, even when he was only a toddler!

"Go on, Booker," Jenny urged him. "Go find Mr. Macauley."

Booker trotted off obediently. Jenny hugged Eliza close for warmth. "Poor little baby," she whispered to Eliza. " No momma to love you."

Eliza sighed contentedly and wrapped her plump fingers around a lock of her sister's hair. She was the happiest little girl Jenny had ever seen, when she should have been the saddest. "But I suppose you are better off than any of us. You don't remember Momma, so you can't miss her."

Eliza's small hand fell idle in her sister's hair. She lay her head down on Jenny's chest, her breathing deep and even. "You little imp," Jenny laughed, "You've gone and fallen asleep!"

She pushed her nose into her sister's hair and inhaled her warm scent. "I promised Momma I'd take care of you and I will, "she whispered.

They'd been at anchor long enough for the sun to begin its slow descent into the western sea. The *Black Diamond* rocked gently on the ebbing tide. Twice the steward, a Scottish man with a brogue as thick as his overworked arms, asked Jenny if she wanted anything, and twice Jenny refused. "I just want to go ashore," she said.

As the tide crept slowly out of Vesuvius Bay, the gap between the *Black Diamond* and Salt Spring Island lessened. It appeared to Jenny that the beach swelled inch by inch, until it almost touched the ship, but she knew this was merely an illusion, and in another twelve hours the fractured shoreline would be submerged again. All their supplies had to be lugged over the rocky beach and up to the cabin. Two canoes, paddled by an Indian couple, ferried between the ship and the land loaded with their boxes and crates.

"I'm not running any more," Jenny swore, rocking Eliza gently. "Momma always had to move, never staying in one spot for long and she hated it. That won't be my life."

"That's right," agreed Booker, "we're not running anymore."

Mr. Macauley strode over to them. "If you're are ready, Jenny," he said, "it's time to disembark."

"Come on, Booker," said Jenny. "Let's go find Daddy. It's time to go home."

SALT SPRING ISLAND:
Originally named Ts'ewaan ("land goes right down to water") by Cowichan- (more properly Island Hul'qumi'num) and Saanich-speaking Coast Salish people. Changed to Salt Spring Island by the Hudson's Bay Company in 1853.

CHAPTER SIXTEEN

*J*enny and the children crossed the beach, moving quickly. Jenny was acutely aware of the need to reach Daddy's cabin before sunset. Finding themselves alone on this strange shore was an unexpected turn of events, but rumors of a dispute between Indians and settlers on the south end of the island had forced Mr. Macauley to reluctantly abandon his charges. "I apologize, Jenny," he said, "but I don't have a lot of choice. I have to go and sort this out before it gets out of hand. You'll have to leave what you can't carry on the beach and make your own way to your Daddy's cabin. I believe the trail is reasonably well-marked."

Jenny carried Eliza, and Booker trailed along behind, half-carrying, half-dragging a potato sack full of their linens. They were thankful that the cattle tracks were easy to follow in the rocky sand, because the bush was so thick they could not have found the entrance to the path on their own. Jenny made a mental note to ask Daddy to place a marker at the foot of the trail.

They entered the forest and found themselves on a crude, narrow trail that wound and climbed through heavy underbrush. Ferns taller than Jenny pushed out of the soft ground on either side of the path. Huge trees covered in bright green mosses towered over their heads, allowing little light. Where the smallest shaft of sunshine penetrated the forest, bushes heavy with berries reached out their brambly branches and made the going even more difficult.

The trail would have been tricky to navigate even if Jenny had been on her own. Carrying Eliza and pulling Booker along beside her made it almost impossible. To make matters worse, fresh piles of cow dung marked the ascent up from the beach.

"Watch where you walk," warned Jenny.

Too late. Booker marched through the cow droppings. "Yuck," he said, and tromped through another pile. "Yuck. Yuck."

What began as a gradual slope grew progressively steeper and more treacherous. *If I were alone, I would sit down and I would cry,* thought Jenny, but she didn't have time to dwell on her discomfort. A sound in the woods stopped them all in their tracks. Jenny's misery turned to fear. She held Eliza tightly and pulled Booker close to her body.

"What's that?" Booker cried. "There's something in the bush! I heard a noise."

"Hush, Booker. I heard it too." Jenny listened, but the woods were quiet. She took a step forward — nothing — and another step. Off to their left a branch snapped. "It's an animal," she said. "It's tracking us, I think. Hush and listen." They listened.

"We need to make plenty of noise, so we scare it off. Eliza, if there ever is a time for you to start up your crying or kick up a fuss, it's now."

"Joseph says there are cougars and bears and wolves here," pointed out Booker. "He says cougars and bears will eat us, and wolves will tear us apart."

Jenny peered nervously into the bush, but the canopy of thick, leafy branches smothered the light. She'd never seen a wolf or a bear, only their skins. They were big and frightening, even when dead.

"Hush, Booker. You're not helping," snapped Jenny. "Joseph is wrong. Nothing is going to eat us. If an animal hears us coming, it'll stay out of our path." She prayed to God she was right. "And don't run, whatever you do," she added. "If it's a big cat, it will chase us down. Let's sing."

They trudged on up the narrow, climbing trail through the heavy bush. Jenny had to stop several times to rest. Eliza had never felt so heavy. Booker and Jenny sang the old songs their momma had taught them — songs about the South and slavery and freedom. Jenny found the familiar lyrics comforting. Finally, when she didn't think she could take another step, they broke out of the forest into a large, messy clearing. Jenny fell to the ground. "Booker, we did it," she said.

"I was never afraid," he replied.

Jenny smiled at him. "Neither was I. Momma was with us."

She looked around the clearing. Stumps five feet across littered the area; some were torn half out of the ground while others remained anchored to the forest floor. At midday the sun would shine here, but in the evening, the light cast a sombre grey shadow on everything. The cattle milled about restlessly, foraging for food, their tails swishing lazily at the flies buzzing around their heads. They too seemed relieved to be at the end of their journey.

"Daddy!" Booker called.

Daddy strode across the middle of the clearing. He stopped beside a large pile of chopped wood and put down the big axe he was carrying. He grinned over at them, but when he saw they were alone, his face clouded.

"Where's your escort? Where are the supplies?"

"Our supplies are still on the beach. Don't worry, I moved them to above the tide line," Jenny said, anticipating Daddy's next question.

Jenny thought Daddy looked tired, older than she remembered. White streaks ran through his black hair. Behind him stood the small, partially finished log cabin he and Joseph had worked so hard to build all summer. The glassless windows stared vacantly out over the lot. A rectangle had been cut for the door. There was no roof. At the edge of the clearing stood a rough lean-to for the cattle.

Home, thought Jenny. *Finally I'm home.*

Booker ran into Daddy's arms. "Daddy!"

"I expected you earlier." He picked up his son, throwing him high into the air. "So you've arrived at last! And on your own! Where's Mr. Macauley?"

"Mr. Macauley had to fix a problem between the Siwash and the settlers!" Booker said, slipping into the Chinook Jargon term for Indians. "But Jenny said she'd come all the way across America and up the coast without him, so a rocky beach and hike up a trail wasn't going to keep her away from home."

Jenny lowered a squirming Eliza to the ground. "It's true," she confirmed, "We were way to close too give up at the very end of our journey."

"Daddy," Eliza cried.

"There's my little girl." Daddy picked up Eliza. "The trail is dangerous if you're unarmed," he spoke to Jenny over Eliza's head. "You're very brave."

"We heard sounds in the bush," she replied, "almost as if something was tracking us. Daddy, can't I learn to shoot?"

Daddy frowned. "I guess so. It's either that or you'll have to spend all your time in the cabin. You're very brave," he repeated. Jenny blushed.

"Joseph," Daddy called.

Joseph stepped out of the forest. He too carried a large axe. He smiled when he saw his sisters and brother and wrapped them all in a bear hug. "Welcome home," he said. "What do you think?"

"It's ours," Jenny replied. "It's our island home." She swallowed back her tears.

Joseph hugged her. "I know," he said. "At last."

"Joseph, get the gun," Daddy interrupted. "Jenny thinks there might have been a cat tracking them up from the beach."

"Lord," Joseph said, "if that's the case, you're lucky to be alive. They come over to pick off our livestock. I've already killed four cougars this summer. They swim over from the mainland. Who would have thought a cat would swim?" He went into the cabin to retrieve his shotgun.

"Will you be fine on your own for a bit, Jenny?" Daddy asked. "I'll go with Joseph to get the supplies on the beach. We don't have long before it's dark."

"I'll be finer when I can shoot," she replied.

"Good girl. I'll get down to the beach right away. Remember Henry Robinson? He'll help me haul the supplies up."

"Henry and Nellie Robinson? Of course I remember them, but I thought they'd settled in Saanich."

"They did, but changed their minds. I think you'll find we know most of the settlers over here. I'm off. Sorry to leave when you've just arrived, but it'll be dark soon. You can explore, but don't wander out of the clearing. There are cat tracks everywhere."

"Come on, Eliza," said Jenny. "We'll go and explore our cabin."

Even though there was no roof, it was dark inside the cabin, but Jenny didn't mind. The sun had begun to sink behind the trees and soon it would be bedtime — their first sleep in their new home. She rummaged around until she found some candles on the plank table. There wasn't much to see — only one room, no windows, holes cut in walls, no door and no roof. The wood stove occupied one corner, a pile of cedar logs stacked neatly beside it. Nearby stood a newly made table flanked by two long rough-hewn benches. Daddy's bedroll snuggled up against one wall, Joseph's against another. A rough cupboard, not yet hung, leaned against the far wall. Three crates —

makeshift chicken coops — occupied the middle of the room.

"Chickens!" Booker poked his finger in through the mesh. The birds retreated to the back of the cage, squawking.

"This must be the safest place for them," said Jenny.

So this was to be their home. She couldn't hide her dismay. How were all five of them going to live here? There would be no privacy and the nights would be freezing.

Jenny sat down heavily on top of a crate of chickens. They squawked and clucked beneath her. Her arms ached from carrying Eliza. She longed to rest.

"I'm hungry," said Booker.

"Oh, Lord," said Jenny.

Would this day ever end?

"As soon as slavery fired upon the flag it was felt, we all felt, even those who did not object to slaves, that slavery must be destroyed. We felt that it was a stain to the Union that men should be bought and sold like cattle … There had to be an end to slavery."

— Ulysses Grant, President of the United States from 1869 to 1877

CHAPTER SEVENTEEN

*O*ver the next few days, Jenny busied herself in the cabin. She nailed a heavy quilt over the doorway so that Eliza couldn't escape and she prepared meals for her family.

"What're you going to put on the roof?" Joseph teased. "A horse blanket?"

"If I were you, I wouldn't tease the cook," Jenny laughed.

Joseph had been unsuccessful in killing the cougar that had stalked them, although he'd seen clear signs of a big cat in the tangled brush that flanked the trail. That was enough for Daddy to decide that, girl or not, Jenny needed to learn to shoot.

"Joseph will teach you how to handle a rifle," he declared, "and I'll buy you your own gun next time I'm at the general store."

Over the next two weeks, Daddy and Joseph worked hard to complete the cabin. They replaced the quilt Jenny had hung with a heavy wooden door and put shakes on the roof. Daddy bought some thick glass for the windows and milled his own planks for the floor. Booker helped Daddy build rustic wooden bed frames for all of them, but Eliza insisted on sleeping with Jenny.

"You're good to your baby sister," Daddy told her. "Momma would be proud of you. I know I am."

Jenny's heart burst with joy.

Gradually, the family fell into a steady routine. Although it was too late in the season to plant, the land had to be cleared, the thousand-year-old trees cut down, the wood split and the reluctant stumps wrenched from the greedy ground. They worked in spite of the heat and mosquitoes. The cows demanded milking morning and night, the water had to be hauled up from the creek, and food kept on the table.

There were plenty of wild animals to hunt, and Booker, Eliza and Jenny cleaned and butchered the deer, rabbits and squirrels Daddy or Joseph hunted. Joseph taught Jenny to shoot, and whenever she had the chance, she practised, taking aim at a block of wood she had nailed to a tree. The big gun recoiled into her shoulder when she fired, but she gritted her teeth around the pain and kept on shooting. She was soon a fine markswoman and no longer felt afraid in the woods alone. Every morning, Jenny took Eliza down to the beach to collect food. At night, the family gorged on the oysters, mussels and clams offered up by the sea.

After a few weeks, Daddy bought ten pigs and six turkeys from a farmer in Saanich and a big dog to keep the cougars and bears away.

"You name him, Jenny," Daddy said. "He seems to like you best of all."

"Archie," Jenny said promptly.

Even though the whole family toiled from dawn to dusk,

they ate a meal together every evening and took the time for Bible-reading before bed.

There were six other colored families carving out farms on Salt Spring Island, all at the north end around Vesuvius Bay. They traded amongst each other, helped each other out and provided much needed entertainment and company. Soon Jenny got to know the other settlers as well, many of whom had taken Coast Salish women for their wives. Jenny came to love these women who had so much knowledge about the land where they lived. They taught her how to shuck oysters without cutting herself, how to smoke deer meat and how to preserve the fresh fish they pulled from the generous ocean.

Joseph worked beside Daddy, just as Jenny had once worked beside her mother as a young slave in Clay County, and later on in California. Now, she found she missed having someone to talk during her chores. When she had five minutes to herself, she read from the family bible.

The lengthy journey from California had changed Daddy. As he aged, he grew more thoughtful. His long days left him little time to play with Booker and Eliza and most nights he fell into bed immediately after dinner, exhausted. He rarely smiled, and spoke even less. Jenny knew he had a lot on his mind, and she guessed he missed Momma now more than ever. In spite of this, she resented his long silences. She was lonely for company.

The fierce winter storms lasted until mid-March and then the rains came. Jenny awoke every morning to heavily overcast skies and a chill that lodged itself in her bones and refused to leave. The rain pounded on the roof. It ran down the windows, and seeped in through the cracks in the loosely chinked walls.

Jenny loved her life on Salt Spring, but she missed the drier climates she'd come from. "In California," she told Booker dreamily, "it hardly ever rains."

The rain made life difficult for everybody. Outside, as the frigid temperature slowly crept up and the winter turned into spring, the animals huddled together in the oozing mud, their tails to the wind, seeking warmth from each other. Inside, the younger children grew restless.

"I can't wait for the schoolhouse to be built," Jenny said to Daddy. "Booker just doesn't want to do his lessons with me, and Eliza is impossible."

"You'll have your schoolhouse by the end of April," promised Daddy. He and the rest of the men had begun work on a one-room school in February.

Once a week, Jenny trekked across the island to the Brodwell store in central Salt Spring to sell her eggs and buy groceries. It was there that she caught up on the gossip and met with the other settlers. And it was there that she met Will Anderson, the Sunday school teacher.

"I like to talk to someone who appreciates book learning," he told her.

"I just like to talk," Jenny replied shyly. Will was a tall, broad-shouldered man in his early twenties. Jenny thought him the most handsome man in the world.

Finally, on April 25, the schoolhouse accepted its first students. It was a cold day and snow blanketed the ground, but that didn't stop the settlers from bundling up and trudging from their homesteads to the schoolhouse, where a fire burned brightly in the wood stove.

The one-room log building doubled as a church on Sundays.

Jenny looked forward to church. Here she felt close to Momma and to Agnes and she got to see the whole community together in one place. Her previous life in Clay County, Missouri now seemed to belong to another person. Her only regret was that Momma hadn't lived to know true freedom.

Will Anderson was hired to teach the children, both during the week and at Sunday school, and he covered every subject from Latin to the sciences. Once a month, weather allowing, the traveling preachers made the risky crossing in flat-bottomed boats from Fort Victoria to Salt Spring Island and everyone looked forward to their sermons and their opinions on news of the outside world.

All the families took turns putting up the different preachers during their stays on the island. Jenny's favorite was Ebenezer Ferris. "He reminds me of Mifflin Gibbs," she told Booker. "Never at a loss for words and always willing to help out."

"If it's fine with you, Jenny," Ebenezer would say, "I'll take Eliza and Booker down to the beach to dig for clams."

"Can we go, Jenny?" the children chorused.

Jenny knew that Ebenezer understood how much she valued her time without the younger ones. On those occasions, she and Will Anderson would walk together in the woods discussing books, or she would practice target shooting. At night, they feasted on fried clams and potatoes thrown into the fire coals.

Daddy liked Will Anderson almost as much as Jenny did. "He's never afraid to pick up an axe or help build a fence," he said with approval. But it was what he didn't say that pleased Jenny the most. Jenny knew that Daddy would accept Will as a son-in-law, if only he would ask for her hand.

One night, Daddy said to Will Anderson, "I'm thinking about making a claim on a small patch of land near the beach. Of course we'll keep the farm, but Jenny and the kids will be safer out of the bush."

"It's a fine idea, Howard," Will agreed. "I worry about Jenny and the children up here all alone."

Jenny's heart skipped a beat. "More coffee?" she offered, jumping up and hurrying to the stove. She didn't want Will to see how pleased she was — on two counts: she was dying of loneliness on the isolated mountainside that she called home; and Will cared something for her.

After Will left, Jenny hoped Daddy would tell her a little more about his plans for moving, but instead he went straight to bed. Still, if there was one thing that she'd learned, it was that once Daddy made a plan, he carried it out. Soon they would live nearer the water.

"Once you let the black man get upon his person the brass letters, U.S., let him get an eagle on his button, and a musket on his shoulder and bullets in his pocket, there is no power on earth that can deny that he has earned the right to citizenship."

— Frederick Douglass, a former slave who became one of the foremost leaders of the abolitionist movement, and one of America's first great black speakers

CHAPTER EIGHTEEN

*D*addy pre-empted beachfront property in the winter of 1860. By August of 1861, he had built a two-room cabin on the new property. The whole community pitched in. Jenny was thrilled when the time came to move, even though she knew she'd be required to travel to the mountain farm on a daily basis to pick fruit and tend the garden.

By the fall, Jenny had something new to worry about. The outside world was intruding yet again. Traveling preachers were confirming what Amor de Cosmos, the well-known journalist, editorialized about in his daily paper that she picked up on her weekly visits to Brodwell store: there was trouble brewing in the United States. One night after Eliza and Booker were in bed, Jenny and Joseph sat up with Will and Daddy. Will was worried and distracted.

"I hear there's talk of a war," he said, "the north against the south. Things aren't good in Fort Victoria, Confederate flags everywhere, and I sense the tides of welcome turning against our people."

Jenny listened, her heart sinking. Last week, Joseph had returned from buying supplies in the Fort, his right eye swollen and purple. "Don't fuss," he said. "There's talk of war in the States, and deserters are flowing into New Caledonia by the boatload."

"But the British are on our side, aren't they?" Jenny asked. "After all, they didn't return Charles Mitchell to his owner, in spite of all the pressure to do just that."

"Who's Charles Mitchell?" asked Booker.

"A runaway slave boy," Jenny explained. "He belonged to James Tilton, from Olympia in Oregon Territory. Charles wanted his freedom so he stowed away on a ship bound for Victoria. When he arrived in port, he was arrested. When Mr. Tilton heard about this, he demanded that Charles be immediately returned to him, but the British refused. They fought Mr. Tilton and eventually granted Charles citizenship. It was considered a huge insult to the Americans, and confirmed what we already know — the British are willing to protect our people."

Will rolled his eyes. "The British are just afraid the Americans are going to steal their land. The only side they are on is their own. They'll protect us for as long as we are useful to their cause and not a second more."

Jenny hoped he was wrong.

"Hope," said Daddy, "never got a house built, or a field planted. No use worrying about what we can't change. There's work to be done." That was Daddy's answer to everything. Work, work, work.

But not even gruelling daily chores could take Jenny's mind off the rumors of civil war in the United States. The young black men who had adopted Canada as their new home talked of nothing but joining the Union Army. Jenny feared she would lose Joseph to a Confederate bullet, and begged him not to enlist.

Joseph kept his thoughts to himself.

Throughout the fall, Jenny and her family ate well on Salt Spring Island, much better fare than they'd ever enjoyed in California. Between their thriving vegetable garden, the young orchard and the wild game and fish, there was never a shortage of mouthwatering food on the table.

But getting the food to the table was backbreaking work and took up all the daylight hours.

In the early mornings when the tide was low, Jenny and Booker raked the beach, pulling in fistfuls of the giant clams that clung to every surface while Eliza threw them into buckets. They made fishing poles out of pliable willow branches, string and bent pushpins, and they traded their corn, carrots, potatoes and homeground flour for fat salmon the Indians caught in the waters off the island.

Jenny had become an excellent shot, and Joseph trapped raccoon, mink and otter all winter long. As well, they got twenty dollars for cougar skins. Daddy taught them to kill only what they could eat or sell or trade at the market, but many of the settlers killed at random. This began to cause enormous problems for the Indians on nearby Kuper Island, who regarded Salt Spring Island as a living grocery store. Suddenly the shelves were emptying: The clams were no longer knee-deep, the oyster beds were depleted and the big game — the bear and the cougar — were becoming scarcer, while deer still roamed the island freely.

Nonetheless, as the months rolled into another year, Jenny's passion for island life grew. Finally she felt she had fulfilled her promise to Momma. Eliza was a happy, well-adjusted little girl, whose earlier tendency to temper-tantrums had been replaced by a sunny, helpful disposition. With Booker and Eliza in school every day, Jenny began to enjoy the freedom she had only dreamed of. Still, she worried about Joseph.

Although the hardships of the civil war in the United States seemed a world away, the black community in the newly declared colony of British Columbia was losing many young men who were returning to the United States to fight on the side of the Yankees for freedom.

Before the year was out, Jenny's worst fear was realized. Joseph had never really settled on the island, not in his heart, and Jenny sensed his restlessness. Only weeks after news reached Fort Victoria of the outbreak of war between the North and the South, Joseph sailed for San Francisco, leaving his family short a strong man, a son and a brother.

"I'll not miss this damn cold," Joseph said as he climbed into the boat. "And I'll be back as soon as we've won," he added.

On the morning that Joseph left, Jenny, Daddy, Eliza and Booker stood on the beach and watched him row away toward the *Black Diamond*. Daddy turned away so nobody would see the tears in his eyes.

None of them said a word about Joseph's empty chair at dinner that night, or the day after, and pretty soon the smaller children stopped asking about him. Jenny knew she'd somehow let Momma down.

Joseph's departure broke Daddy's heart all over again, even if he tried to keep it to himself. He still mourned Agnes and Hannah, so much so that he refused to consider taking another wife. Jenny broached the topic gently on several occasions. "I'll always stay loyal to your momma," he'd reply and he wouldn't say another word about it — just go back to pulling stumps or plowing the rocky soil, until exhaustion brought on sleep.

The first few letters home from Joseph were discouraging. The Northern army refused to enlist black men, and flatly turned down their offers to fight to end slavery. Only the Navy would accept black sailors, but Joseph wanted to be in the infantry.

"We could use his help here," complained Daddy. "The farm is too much for one man, a girl and two children. I need a man to live on the mountain property or we risk losing it."

Under the rules of pre-emption, the land had to be occupied and under improvement, or it reverted back to the government. There were plenty of settlers who would have loved to get their hands on that land, so Daddy enlisted the help of an acquaintance who'd come up from Placerville to work in Victoria: Ezra Grant. He was soon installed in the mountain cabin and Jenny no longer had to make the daily trek up the steep path to the orchard and grazing lands.

Jenny disliked Ezra the first time she laid eyes on his big, muscular frame and noted his narrow darting eyes, but she kept her thoughts to herself. Daddy couldn't do the work alone.

Will Anderson came for dinner on a warm evening in late April. Jenny noticed his thoughtful mood, but knew better than to ask what was troubling him. She knew he'd talk when he was ready. After she'd cleared the table and served coffee, he spoke.

"There's been a massive gold strike on the Salmon River," he said. "Gold miners are pouring in from San Francisco once again."

"That's good news for the merchants," offered Jenny.

"So many people coming here at once puts a lot of pressure on the law and on the land," retorted Will. "In my opinion, the colony is growing too fast. I worry about you, Jenny — you and the young ones. You need someone strong to be with you on your homestead."

Jenny blushed and hurried away to do the dishes. *If I have to marry someone*, she thought, *I'll marry that man.*

By the President of the United States of America:

A PROCLAMATION

Whereas on the 22nd day of September, A.D. 1862, a proclamation was issued by the President of the United States, containing, among other things, the following, to wit:

"That on the 1st day of January, A.D. 1863, all persons held as slaves within any State or designated part of a State the people whereof shall then be in rebellion against the United States shall be then, thenceforward, and forever free; and the executive government of the United States, including the military and naval authority thereof, will recognize and maintain the freedom of such persons and will do no act or acts to repress such persons, or any of them, in any efforts they may make for their actual freedom …

And I hereby enjoin upon the people so declared to be free to abstain from all violence, unless in necessary self-defense; and I recommend to them that, in all case when allowed, they labor faithfully for reasonable wages.

And I further declare and make known that such persons of suitable condition will be received into the armed service of the United States to garrison forts, positions, stations, and other places, and to man vessels of all sorts in said service.

And upon this act, sincerely believed to be an act of justice, warranted by the Constitution upon military necessity, I invoke the considerate judgment of mankind and the gracious favor of Almighty God."

CHAPTER NINETEEN

Will Anderson finished reading the relevant paragraphs of the Emancipation Proclamation. He grinned across the table at Jenny. "The cynics among us say Lincoln did this because he is running low on soldiers to fight the Confederates. That might be the case for the moment, but history will thank him for this. The black man will be a fine soldier."

Joseph had sent the whole document in a letter along with the news that he had become a member of America's first-ever all-black fighting regiment: the 54th Massachusetts.

"It's commanded by Colonel Robert Shaw, and he is a fine man, though not one to cross," Joseph wrote. "This might be my last letter for a time as we are off to South Carolina to fight our first battle as a unit."

"I pray he'll be safe," Jenny said.

"We'll say prayers in church for the whole regiment," Will replied.

If it wasn't for Will Anderson, Jenny mused, she might have lost her mind. One day not long after their conversation about

Joseph's letter, she found herself confiding in Will about Ezra.

"What is it you don't like about him?" Will asked.

"I just don't trust him," Jenny replied.

"Can you be a little more specific, girl?'

"I don't like the way he looks at me for one thing," Jenny said shyly.

"Have you talked to your daddy about this?" Will sounded agitated. Jenny wasn't sure who was making him angrier — herself or Ezra or Daddy.

"It's really nothing," she said. "Let's return to our studies."

They were sitting at the kitchen table in Will's small one-room cabin. Outside, the incessant rain turned the forest a deep green, but the cold moist air promised snow.

Inside, the wood stove burned under a pot of boiling coffee. Will took two cups and filled them with the warm grainy drink. He said nothing, but the vein in the front of his forehead throbbed and his mouth was set in a tight line.

"Will," Jenny said. "I should never have brought this up. Don't you go over-reacting and causing trouble." She smiled tentatively at the schoolteacher. "He helps out Daddy and we couldn't do without him on the mountain."

"That's not the point," replied Will. "The point is a young woman like yourself, pretty as a picture and smart as a whip, shouldn't be sharing space with a man like Ezra."

"I can take care of myself," sniffed Jenny. "I've been doing a fine job for years, and looking after the younger ones too. I'm sorry I brought it up at all."

"Well, I'm not. Look at me, Jenny Estes." Will leaned over

the table and cupped Jenny's chin in his large hand. She flushed all the way from her head to her toes. "Will you consider taking me as your husband?"

"Are you …?" Jenny's heart thumped in her chest. She'd dreamed about this moment in her most private thoughts, but she never thought it would come true. There was no doubt in her heart that she loved Will, and in that second she knew that there was no doubt in her mind either. "I would consider it an honor," she replied.

Will exhaled and covered his hand over hers.

For a minute her world looked perfect, but than reality crashed in. "I would consider it an honor," she said slowly, "but I'm obligated to Eliza and Booker and even to Daddy. I made a promise to my momma …" She felt a heavy sadness, pushed it away. No man would want to marry a girl with so many responsibilities.

Will didn't move his hand, didn't hesitate for a second. Instead he flashed his white teeth at her. "I thought I'd build us our own little cabin right beside the one you're in now, so you could be with the kids after we are married, and your daddy can always use another strong man."

"Yes," said Jenny finding herself wordless for the first time in her memory. "Yes. Lord, I don't know what to say!"

"Nothing more to say," laughed Will. "I'm going to walk you home, and we'll tell everyone our news, and we'll plan a wedding, the finest wedding party ever."

Kissing Will seemed about the best thing Jenny had ever done.

"*I urge you to fly to arms and smite with death the power that would bury the government and your liberty in the same hopeless grave.*"

— Frederick Douglass

CHAPTER TWENTY

The whole community got together to build Jenny and Will a little bedroom off the main beach cabin. It was a wonderful wedding gift, and one they appreciated more than anyone knew. And when Will joined the family, Ezra was let go, much to Jenny's relief.

Marriage suited Jenny. Her life didn't really change that much, except that last thing at night before she closed her eyes, and first thing at dawn when she opened them, Will was beside her. Within three months of their wedding, she found herself expecting a child.

There had been nothing, not a single word, from Joseph for a long while, and then two letters arrived, one on the heels of the other. Jenny's fingers trembled when she opened the first envelope and glanced over the plain, white paper. Joseph had never been a scholar, but his handwriting was shaky and more difficult to read than she remembered.

"Go on, read it," said Daddy. "What does he say?"

All of them had gathered around the kitchen table. Will and

even Ezra had been summoned the second the letters were delivered by the boat from Victoria. Jenny looked at Will and smiled. She suspected he'd had words with Ezra, whose behavior toward her had gone from disrespect to something akin to fear.

"*February, 1863. Dear Daddy, Jenny and kids,*" Jenny began.

I will tell you that I am well, but that there is smallpox in our regiment. There is thousands of poor soldiers who will never see home again. Our regiment, the 54th Massachusetts, is one to be proud of. Many of the men are free men or runaway slaves. Will was right: we are fine soldiers every last one of us.

Our commander is a good man, and only twenty-five years old. He is white, but takes kindly to all of us and treats us as equals, as long as we don't break army rules. We are paid seven dollars a month, but often we do not receive our wages. They is less than the white boys by a long way, but we is told the pay will go up. There is no food to buy here or nothing so I save my wages. We make our own liquor and pour it down the throats of the dying. Here is the recipe: bark juice, tar-water, turpentine, brown sugar, lamp oil and alcohol. It offers some comfort.

If you saw the sick and dying soldiers it would make your heart ache. Pray for me and hope I do not fill the grave of a coward.

Your loving Son and Brother,
Joseph

"Go on and read the next letter," Daddy said.

"It's penned five months later," Jenny said. "July of 1863."

"*Dear Daddy and Jenny and kids,*

I welcome Will into our family. He is a fine man. I wish I knew him better.

I am shot in the thigh at Fort Wagner and do not expect to return home to you. We have lost over 200 men and come back only 400 with many wounded. But we done a good job and attacked the Confederate Fort, even if we didn't outright win. I am sad to say that Colonel Shaw is shot dead. Here is the citation:

'When the color sergeant was shot down, this soldier grasped the flag, led the way to the parapet, and planted the colors thereon. When the troops fell back he brought off the flag, and under fire in which he was twice severely wounded.'

You'll never guess, but Frederick Douglass' son died in the battle too. You recall I liked what he said about the war and that partly caused me to join.

The battle was terrible wet and muddy and the Confederates fired upon us something fierce. Already we are fifty-four dead and more will die.

I am not afraid, but I wish I could see you all once more before I go to Momma and my sister and heaven.

Your loving son and brother, who believes that love is deathless,

Joseph"

Jenny read the last letter slowly, fighting to keep her voice steady. When she'd finished, she passed it over to Daddy. Even though he couldn't read, he spread the letter out in front of him and sat and stared at it for eternity. Will stood up, gripped Daddy's shoulder and went outside.

"Come on, Booker and Eliza," he said. "I could use a little help on the boat, and Ezra, you go on up to the mountain and get the cows in." He turned to Jenny. "Don't expect us until dinner," he said.

When they'd all left, Jenny boiled a pot of coffee and set down a steaming cup in front of Daddy. He ran his finger around the brim of the cup absently, but Jenny saw by his eyes that he was a thousand miles away on a union battlefield with his dying son.

Finally he spoke. "It seems that no matter what I do to change the fate of this family, we are bound to die on American soil. Sometimes, more and more often now, I've been dreaming about going south. It's in the back of my mind that if President Lincoln wins this war, I just might go home one day."

"The living are here," Jenny replied. "Will and Eliza and me and the baby — we need you. Don't think about …" She stopped, realizing she was about to say *Don't think about running off again.* It was a phrase Momma might have used, *had* used so often when Daddy got wanderlust. "Don't think about tomorrow. Think about what we have to do today. It's easier that way."

"I know it," Daddy said. "I think what I might do is to take a little walk and put some thoughts into Joseph." The words caught in his throat and he paused for a long minute.

"He would have gone fighting, no matter what," Jenny said.

"I know," said Daddy. "It doesn't make it any easier, though. I'm proud of him, but he's still gone from us." He wiped a tear from his eye. "Agnes, Hannah and now Joseph. So much lost."

Jenny watched him shuffle slowly out the door of the cabin.

She stood for a long time after he'd left and tried to remember what it had been like before all the dying began. Inside her, she felt the baby move.

Jenny pulled on her overcoat and walked down to the shoreline. In the distance she saw Will, Eliza and Booker working on the boat, but they didn't see her, so engrossed were they in their repairs.

She followed the trail to the Rubbing Rocks where the great whales came in at high tide to scrape barnacles off their backs. She watched an eagle circle in the air current above her, soaring and diving on the invisible wind.

"Goodbye, Joseph," she whispered.

There was so much she still didn't understand. But now one more life was over, and yet another was about to begin.

HISTORICAL NOTE

*T*his story was inspired by the experiences of Sylvia Stark who settled on Salt Spring Island in 1860. Thanks to her daughter, the late Marie Albertina Stark for taking the time to record her mother's life story in such detail.

ACKNOWLEDGEMENTS

I would like to thank the following people for their help with this novel:

Lynn Henry for walking beside me through the long process of turning a manuscript into a book.

Brian Thom, PhD, for sharing his expertise on West Coast Native/Indigenous language and culture.

Wayde Compton, Rod McFarland and James Moffat for their careful reading and evaluation of this manuscript.

Patrick Burke for his astute fact checking.

Helen Godolphin for her meticulous editing.

And, of course, my publisher, Michelle Benjamin at Raincoast Books for her ongoing support and encouragement.

DID YOU KNOW?

- One third of the cowboys who built the American West were black.
- One of the first gold discoveries made in the West was by Henry Parker, a black mine owner.
- In 1849 twenty-five thousand pioneers migrated East to California.
- Not all migrants could afford a wagon, a yoke or even a horse. So they wheel-barrowed their way across the Plains.
- In 1858, Bill 339 was passed prohibiting the emigration of "free Negroes" and "other obnoxious persons" into the state of California.
- In 1858, between six to eight hundred black emigrants left California and sailed to British Columbia where they settled on Vancouver Island and Salt Spring Island.
- British Columbia's first police force consisted entirely of black emigrants from California. The sixty-member unit was called "The Victoria Pioneers Rifle Corps," or "The African Rifles."
- The terrorist organization known as the Ku Klux Klan preyed on African Americans during the 1800s, but the group did not formalize until after the civil war (1865).

- In 1859, the *Clothilde* arrived in Mobile Bay, Alabama. She was the last slave-ship to arrive on American soil.
- 186,000 African American soldiers fought in the Union Army.
- In 1865, Congress passed the Thirteenth Amendment to the Constitution, abolishing slavery in the United States.
- With the end of the American Civil War, in 1865, half of the original black settlers in Canada returned to the United States.
- On the December 12, 1867, Mifflin Gibbs was elected to Victoria City Council. He was the first African American to be elected to politics in Canada and he went on to become the first black judge.
- African Americans were denied the right to vote until the Voting Rights Act of 1965.
- Chinook jargon is a creole language based on Chinook, other Native languages, French and English. It was spoken in the northwestern United States and on the Pacific coast of Canada and Alaska.

FURTHER READING

The history of North America is rich with stories about black pioneers. The following books and websites were invaluable to me in my research. This list is not conclusive, nor is it meant to be. I've included it here for readers who want to further explore this fascinating subject.

Women and Men on the Overland Trail, Faragher, John Mack (Yale University Press, 2000)

Go Do Some Great Thing, Kilian, Crawford (Douglas & McIntyre, 1978)

The Negro Trail Blazers of California, Beasley, Delilah (Los Angeles, 1919)

Early Negro Settlement in Victoria, Pilton, James W., Master Thesis, University of British Columbia, 1951

Incidents in the Life of a Slave Girl, Jacobs, Harriet A., Boston 1861

The Diary of Sylvia Stark as told to her daughter Marie Albertina Stark, Salt Spring Island Archives, Add. Mss. 91. WALLACE, Marie Albertina (Stark), 1867-1966, Salt Spring Island, B.C.

Shadow and Light: an autobiography, Gibbs, Mifflin Wistar, New York: Arno Press, 1968

Who killed William Robinson? Race, Justice and Settling the Land— A Historical Whodunit, http://web.uvic.ca/history-robinson/

Black History: A Vancouver Public Library Guide, History & Government Division, 2001

USEFUL WEBSITES

Africans in America: www.pbs.org/wgbh/aia/home.html
Black American West Museum and Heritage Center:
    www.blackamericanwest.org/
British Columbia Archives: www.bcarchives.gov.bc.ca
Dictionary.com: dictionary.reference.com/
HistoryLink: www.historylink.org
Hudson's Bay Employee's Dictionary of Chinook Jargon:
    www.geocities.com
Merriam Webster Online: www.m-w.com/

JULIE BURTINSHAW
is the author of three previous
books: *Dead Reckoning, Adrift,*
and *Romantic Ghost Stories.* She is
a full-time writer living with her
family in Vancouver.

"The strong descriptive writing [shipwrecks] inspire
can often lure reluctant readers into cliff-hanging
stories and the thrall of good writing ... The book's
true facts drive the reader on. The book is hard for any
reader to resist." — *National Post*

**Shortlisted for a Red Cedar Award, Chocolate Lily
Award and Diamond Willow Award.**

"A timely and gritty story into which the author
weaves an exciting subplot ... With its quick pacing
and interesting detail, this book will be popular with
children, including reluctant readers."

— *School Library Journal*

**Shortlisted for the Canadian Library Association
Book of the Year, Chocolate Lily Award and
Manitoba Young Reader's Choice Award.**